TUCUMCARI

Patrick Parks

Patrick Parks (signature)

To Jo + Phil —
I hope you enjoy the book! Let's
get together and talk about foreign
lands.
I f you're ever in Tucumcari,
you've got a place to stay!
— Pat

KERNPUNKT PRESS

Cover Art: "Dorcas Parks" by W.E. Parks
Book Design: Jesi Buell

1st Printing: 2018

ISBN-13 978-0-9972924-6-6

KERNPUNKT Press
701 State Route 12B
Hamilton, New York 13346

www.kernpunktpress.com

for my parents

...the products of his imagination
appear so necessary and natural that
he regards them, and would like them
to be regarded by others, not as
creations of thought,
but as given realities.

-Albert Einstein

Nothing is too wonderful to be true.
                              -Michael Faraday

In the City of Perpetual Snow

One morning in June, I wake up and remember I have a wife. I should say I remember believing I have a wife. Why this occurs to me after so long is a mystery.

On this morning in June, I wake up to a snowstorm. It is not really snow but ash as powdery and white as snow. Swirling from the tops of the tall chimneys of the factories just beyond my neighborhood, the ash drifts down, covering cars and clinging to the shoulders of summer shirts.

If I lie flat on my bed and look out the window, all I can see is the sky. If I prop myself up on pillows, I can see the sky and the hills people around here call mountains. If I sit up completely, I can no longer see the sky, but I can see the hills and the smokestacks of the factories that tower above this city.

I look out the window. The sky is overcast. Snow swirls in the air. Snowy ash swirls in the air. The factories nearby blow the ash out of their tall smokestacks, and it falls like snow, drifts like snow, needs to be shoveled off the sidewalks like snow. All year long, you can hear the scrape of shovels on cement.

*

I came to this city and ended up teaching English to immigrants who came to this city to work in the factories. I teach them how to speak to the people who can give them the jobs they want. They are good students. They are eager to learn and very polite. No matter what I say, they try to repeat it.

"This is soap," I tell them, holding up a pink bar.

"Soap." They all say it together.

"This is a key. Sweater. Pear. Wallet. Nail clippers."

I teach them phrases, too, phrases I think will come in handy.

"How are you today?"

"Could you direct me to the lavatory?"

"How much is this window fan?"

"Sure, I'd be happy to take you there. Hop in."

*

My students are all from different places. They have different hairstyles and wear different kinds of jewelry and shoes. But they are all serious, which I like. They watch each other, sometimes moving their mouths silently along with the one who is speaking, and then nod, smiling, if the person got it right.

2

I used to have a dream about this kind of thing when I was a child. I dreamed I couldn't understand anybody I met, and I didn't know anybody, either. Everyone was a stranger. I didn't like the dream particularly, but I had it a lot.

*

I wake up one morning remembering I have a wife.

I wake up one morning believing I have a wife. I believe I remember a wedding. The ring on my left hand, a simple gold band, seems to confirm that belief.

The woman I believe I am married to is named Audrey. She is tall and rawboned—rangy, I think, is another suitable modifier, or angular, something like that—and she wears her red hair loose, occasionally pulled back with a strip of rawhide or a ribbon. She favors cowboy boots and jeans and men's work shirts but, when she wants, she can cut a striking figure in a sleeveless dress or an evening gown. She is a woman of the West: tough as leather, durable as a cactus. In Tucumcari, where she lives, she throws pots, perhaps, or owns a small ranch just outside of town; it doesn't matter. She might even paint landscapes or have inherited a cafe where dust-caked cowhands come in for a breakfast of Navajo flat bread, eggs Mexican-style, and strong black coffee.

The only jewelry Audrey wears is a wedding band, silver and plain, just like mine.

3

I lie in bed, watch snowy ash swirl against the sky — which is becoming bruise-colored: yellow and purple, like a fading shiner — listen to the slow scrape of a shovel below my window and remember Audrey. I am in no hurry this morning. I am feeling languid — no, languorous. The day is languid.

I'm going to Tucumcari to see Audrey. She doesn't know I'm coming.

I have a postcard from Tucumcari on my refrigerator. The postcard shows a street at night. All you can see are neon lights advertising motels with vacancies: The Palomino, The Apache, The Dusty Trail, The Highway Inn, The Blue Swallow, The Pow Wow Inn. On the back of the card, it says that Tucumcari has more than 2000 motel rooms.

I'm not sure what I'll find when I get there, but I know I'll have a place to stay.

*

The sky has changed color again. Sunlight is breaking through the clouds, which have gone from bruise-colored to a kind of blue-gray.

In sunlight, it is easy to see that the ash swirling outside is ash and not snow. In bright sunlight, snowflakes turn into diamonds. Ash stays white and opaque.

The sun has broken through the clouds completely now,

and I can feel my energy increasing, which backs up the doctor's notion that my trouble is, in part, phototropic. The more light there is, the stronger I feel. I read someplace that every second of every day, 4.3 pounds of sunlight strike the earth. It's no wonder I feel safe and solid during the daytime. I am held down by all that light.

At night, I am so weak, I float. For that reason, I can't sleep with more than one window open; a good cross-breeze and I'm drifting over rooftops.

*

Let me tell you some more about Audrey and me. Here is what I remember happening: We met in Las Vegas. We were both very drunk. When I ran out of money at the blackjack table, she gave me a $5 chip, which I lost on the next hand. She said to me, "I've never seen anybody with such shitty luck in my whole life." "Don't I know it," I said. Then, somehow (this is pretty hazy because, at the time, all of the weightlessness was in my head), we ended up in a wedding chapel.

The next morning, she was gone, but she had left fifty dollars in chips on the nightstand. I went downstairs and lost it all in fifteen minutes because I thought eight was my lucky number.

I remember her saying to me, "Let's get married. I'm going to Tucumcari, and that's a tough place to be single."

"All right," I remember saying, "all right. Maybe it'll change my luck."

I was not surprised when Audrey was gone the next morning. It seemed right at the time but now I am anxious to see her again. When I walk into the restaurant or into the studio where she is weaving rugs or making jewelry or pottery, or when I come across her fixing a fence or behind the desk at the motel she owns, she will brush a strand of her long red hair away from her face and smile at me.

"You made it," she will say. "You finally made it."

"Yes," I'll say. "I finally made it."

This Perfect World

I live in a neighborhood of men. Mostly sad men. Sad-looking men. They don't greet each other on the street. They don't meet each other's eyes. Every morning, I watch them come out of their buildings and head to work. Some, those dressed in blue or brown or gray jumpsuits and carrying lunch buckets walk off in the direction of the factory district. Those dressed in blue or brown or gray suits and carrying battered briefcases line up at the bus stop to be carried away from the factories to the city's office district. Some of these men, some of the ones who work in offices, carry umbrellas to keep the ash from ruining their suits. But most of them don't bother.

*

Across the street from me is a man who never leaves his apartment. I can see down into his apartment from my window. I watch him almost every day. He sits in front of a television set and works jigsaw puzzles on a card table. At night, the light from the television set makes him look blue. In the apartment next to the man who works the puzzles is a man who stands at his window every morning with a cigarette and a cup of coffee. He smokes the cigarette and sips the coffee and looks off toward the city's office district. When he finishes the cigarette, he drops it into the cup and turns away. A few minutes later, I see him coming out of his building. He opens his umbrella and walks to the bus stop.

*

All of the businesses in this neighborhood are men's businesses. Businesses for men. A barber shop, a tobacco shop, a small grocery store that only stocks simple-to-prepare food, a dry cleaner/laundry, a liquor store, a butcher shop, a haberdashery, a used car lot, places like those. Other places like those.

There are women who work in some of these businesses, but they are silent and stern and don't wait on customers. At night, they gather at the bus stop and stand in a cluster with their backs together, vigilant. I don't know where they go when the bus arrives and they all get on. Maybe there's a neighborhood where only women live. I've never heard of such a thing, but it could be true. There could be such a neighborhood.

Occasionally, at night, a car, either dark or light in color, will come into the neighborhood and a woman will get out. She will be short or tall, blonde or wearing a hat. Her coat may be fur. It may be a long coat, with a belt. After checking the address on a card she carries, she will lean in and say something to the driver and then enter one of the apartment buildings. When she is inside, I study the darkened windows overlooking the street and see signs that others are watching, too: a fleeting shadow, the red glow of a cigarette, blind slats parted, curtains pulled aside, a hand pressed against the glass.

The car remains at the curb. If it's cold, the driver will keep it running. If not, he will shut off the engine. I wonder what he does while he waits, if he reads or listens to the radio or sleeps. I wonder if he enjoys what he does and how he got the job. It's a job I might like, especially the waiting part.

*

I bought a car before I knew I would be going to Tucumcari, before I knew I would be leaving this town, this apartment, this bed. It is a station wagon, a very large station wagon, with wood-grained contact paper along the sides. The paper is peeling in spots and there is some rust—there is, actually, quite a bit of rust. But I have been assured the car is sound.

I can't say why I bought the car. Like so many things lately, I don't think about what I have done until afterward. I feel like my whole life exists outside of time somehow. If I tried hard enough, I could probably predict the future. I could see everything that was going to happen before it happened, and I could see what my reaction would be when it was over. That would help me explain why I will have done so many of the things I have yet to do.

It still will not help me explain why I bought the car.

*

It has been a long time since I have driven anywhere. The six blocks between the car lot and here helped me remember how it feels behind the wheel, but the size of the car has me worried.

When I drove regularly, it was always small cars. They were little capsules, hardly big enough for two, but reliable and simple. My station wagon, on the other hand, is fully equipped with gadgets. The ashtray is lighted. The windows go down with the push of a button. Another button moves the seat, and there's another to send up the antenna. I have not driven the car since I bought it, but I have sat in it, learning how to run everything and getting used to the feel of it.

It feels indestructible.

*

My parents owned a station wagon. I would ride way in

the back, lying on pillows and reading, whenever we moved to a new place. If I stood the suitcases on end against the back of the seat, I could not be seen from the front, and I would pretend I had stowed away on a ship. Wherever we ended up, though, was never a place I would want to stow away to, and we moved so many times I stopped trying to remember the names of all the places we lived.

*

One of the places we lived was here, in this city. We lived in a different neighborhood, of course, one with families and yards.

*

I need to practice driving if I'm going to go to Tucumcari. I will need to practice driving, and I will need to plan my route. My way out of the neighborhood and out of the city will take me past the factories, past sewage ponds and landfills and auto salvage yards. It will also take me past the houses of the people who work in the factories and the auto salvage yards. I may recognize some of these people when I drive by because they may be my students. My old students. My former students. They might be standing out in front of a tired tarpaper house. They might be standing on the concrete steps that lead up to the front door of that house from a packed dirt yard. They might look up from under the hood of a

11

car they are fixing with parts stolen from the salvage yards.

If I recognize any of them, I will wave. Maybe they will recognize me and wave back. Maybe they will recognize me and not wave back because they are ashamed to be seen living this way, in these awful houses in this place where the ash is mixed with a fine, rusty dust and the smell is alive and awful, and the children, powdered with rust and ash, already look old.

Still, because I am so happy to be going, I will roll down my window.

"Top of the morning to you," I might say, saluting with two fingers like we practiced in class. "A fine day for this time of year, wouldn't you say?"

If they remember, they will answer, "Couldn't be better."

But there's no reason to think they will remember. Even though the students were always enthusiastic, I hardly ever saw the same faces more than twice.

I hope they will remember me, though. I hope they will remember my face.

*

Even though I have never driven through the factory district, even though I have never been to the factory district, I know what it is like. I know what to expect.

*

Trucks with tires taller than my car, trucks blackened and hardened by smelting fire, rumble away from the factories, a shower of sparks trailing after like the tail of a comet. The cabs are too high for me to see the drivers, but I wave, anyway. This close to the smokestacks, the ash is thick as fog, and I must run the windshield wipers and turn on the headlights. I slow at a cross street, unable to see traffic coming at me from either side, unable to see until nearly too late another of the tall black trucks bearing down on me. I slam my foot against the brake pedal, and the car slides on the ashy drift, slides toward the black knobbed tires, tires as wide as my car, tires that toss up more powder as the truck thunders past, missing me, missing my car.

*

The factories are made of red brick. The factories are made of red brick, and they crowd the street to my right and to my left, and they disappear above my head in the swirling cloud of ash. There are no windows in the factories, only a few steel doors punched into the brick. I see no one going in or out of the steel doors. I see no one out on the narrow sidewalk between the street and the wall. I see no one at all.

Inside these factories are huge blast furnaces. Inside the huge blast furnaces, the temperature is nearly 3000 degrees Fahrenheit. If a man fell into one of the furnaces or walked into one of the furnaces, he would be turned to ash instantly. One of my students who worked in one of the factories told me about the furnaces. He told me a little about the furnaces using the words I had taught him. "Very, very hot. It is hot like hell," he said. I didn't teach him the word *hell*. I don't know where he learned that one. The skin of the man's face was crinkled from the heat and his lips were white with blisters and his eyebrows were gone. Like everybody else in the class, he stopped coming after a while, too. But he came longer than most, and I miss seeing him, even though I didn't like looking at him.

*

Once I'm past the tarpaper houses and my former students, once they're in my rearview mirror and getting smaller, it will be wide highways and open countryside all the way to Tucumcari.

*

I have kept most of my things in boxes since moving to this city. My clothes I unpacked, of course, and kitchen utensils, shaver, items I use daily, but books and souvenirs, my father's letters, my mother's stories, photographs, my parents' ashes, these things I left sealed in the boxes I put them in before I came here. I only have to empty my dresser and medicine cabinet into a suitcase, strip the bed and stuff the sheets, along with towels, into a pillowcase, put my coffeepot and alarm clock, my radio, binoculars, my boots and my heavy winter coat into an empty box, put my typewriter back into its case, and I'm ready to go.

I am used to being ready to go. I am used to leaving and going and arriving and leaving.

Even though I'm used to leaving and getting someplace else, I still need a reason to get moving. I need a push to get me started. Staying put is easy.

*

When I get to Tucumcari, I'm staying put. I'm unpacking everything and throwing away the boxes. I'm going to put things in drawers and on shelves and hang things on the walls and never leave. Never.

*

Audrey didn't leave me a note when she left Las Vegas. She just left me $50 in chips, which I lost at the roulette table.

If Audrey had left me a note, it would have been on that narrow hotel stationery the maids leave next to the telephone.

If Audrey had left me a note, it would have said, *Hey, Darling! If you're ever in Tucumcari, you've got a place to stay. Your loving wife, Audrey.*

If Audrey had left me a note, I'd still be carrying it in my wallet.

If Audrey had left me a note, I'd have cashed in the chips and taken a bus to Tucumcari.

If Audrey had left me a note, I'd be in Tucumcari right now.

I'd be in Tucumcari watching the sun come up over the desert. I'd be drinking coffee from one of those speckled blue tin mugs and looking at the sky turn pink. "Audrey," I'd say. "Come on out. You've got to see this." And she would come out and we'd watch the sun come up together, both of us drinking coffee, happy to be alive on such a glorious day, such a wonderful and perfect day.

How to Survive in the Desert

Before I get to Tucumcari, I need to get myself ready for the heat and light of the desert. Here in this city of perpetual snow, even in the summer months, there is a memory of winter, a thin thread of icy air you can sometimes feel if you walk through it, just as you might wade into a current coming down from the pole when you're in the ocean or step next to a cold spring feeding the lake where you're vacationing with your family. But in the desert, there is no winter, no cold. It is always hot, and the sun burns white in an always cloudless sky.

*

In the library, I found a book about the desert and what to expect. Most of the book was about the plants that live there, the animals and the people, rock formations and so forth, but one section told about staying alive in that unforgiving climate.

When driving through the desert, the road seems endless. There is nothing around for miles and miles. Nothing but desert plants, dry sand and heat. If your car breaks down and you find yourself stuck in the desert, do not panic. You can survive until someone stops to help you or you make it to the next town on your own.

Here's how to do it:

1. Drink lots of water. To do this, you must have brought lots of water with you because you won't find any in the desert. Plan ahead!

2. Take along small nutritious food. Nuts or beef jerky are good, but they will make you thirsty.

3. Wear light-colored clothing that will reflect sunlight and allow you to be seen at night. Though it is unlikely that anyone will stop for you in the desert after dark, at least they will see you and not run over you.

4. Prepare for sand storms. Take along goggles and a bandana. A gas mask works, too.

5. Cross the desert at night. It's cooler, but be careful (see #3).

6. Stay warm. Even though you are in the desert, if you are walking at night, you could freeze to death, so bring along a down jacket or a nice wool sweater. A hat is a good idea, too.

7. Be wary of nocturnal animals. Here is a list:
    a. Coyotes
    b. Wolves
    c. Javelinas

d. *Spiders and scorpions*

e. *Rattlesnakes*

Note: singing will keep most of these creatures away, but it may attract them to you as well.

Above all, keep your wits about you. Remind yourself that you are more than capable and that you will soon be reunited with your loved ones and have a wonderful story to tell them. Make it an adventure!

True Stories about Tucumcari

This is an Apache legend explaining how Tucumcari got its name:

Once there was a beautiful Indian princess named Tocom, and she was in love with a handsome young brave named Kari. A rival for Tocom's affection lured Kari into a fight and killed him with a knife. Tocom got a hold of the knife and killed her beloved's killer, then stabbed herself with it. When her father, the chief, found the bodies of his daughter and the young brave she loved, he shouted, "Tocom, Kari!" and then plunged the knife into his own heart.

*

I found out, too, that some people give the Comanches credit for naming the place. In that language there's a word, *Tukamukaru*, which means, "to lie in wait for someone or something to approach."

20

*

Before the name of the town was changed to reflect the surrounding Native American culture, Tucumcari was a railroad town known as Six Shooter Siding because of its dangerous nature. Gunslingers were everywhere. Outlaws of the vilest nature, violent men with short tempers, roamed the town, shooting each other for no reason other than the delight of hearing the thunder of their pistols and the smell of burnt powder, the thrill of living through another confrontation. Worst and most feared of the lot was Tuscaloosa Tom, the Alabama Bad Man. He was a mad dog, a growling, foaming-at-the-mouth demon who shot so many and shot so often that the barrel of his Colt glowed red and smoldered in his holster.

*

Tucumcari is located in the eastern part of New Mexico, a little north of midway between the borders of Colorado and Texas/Mexico. Just to the south of the city is Playa Largo, a thirty-mile stretch of stone, smooth as a table. It is believed that the Ute Indians discovered flight there. In the desert north of Tucumcari, there is an ancient pinon tree. It hangs on the rim of a ravine with its bare roots holding like talons to the rock. The tree is well-known because during thunderstorms St. Elmo's Fire will engulf it in flames that can be seen for miles.

The Canadian River, which is also north of the city, is the only waterway in North America where cut-lip sturgeon can be found, and nearby Tucumcari Mountain is home to three varieties of poisonous snakes.

*

Tucumcari is the birthplace of a number of well-known individuals including naturalist John Muir, writer Ken Kesey, singer Patti Page, socialite Ruby Woodbridge, boxer Gene Tunney, and musician Stan Getz. A young Georgia O'Keefe spent a month in Tucumcari where she worked as an usher at the opera house.

*

Temperatures in Tucumcari can get as high as 125 degrees in July and rarely go below 80, even in January. Truck farming is significant but no major crops are grown in the area. Cattle ranches abound, as do emu and ostrich ranches. Sheep do not do well in the high desert heat and chickens cannot tolerate the dry air. Water is so scarce that ranchers drill, on average, two wells a week, oftentimes hitting oil rather than water.

*

Before interstate highways, when motorists traveling Route 66 on their way to California hit the open desert, Tucumcari was the only place to stay between Abilene, Texas, and Albuquerque.

At night, with all its neon motel signs lit up, the place was as bright as Las Vegas. To anyone arriving at night, having spent a whole day in a hot car, the place must have looked like heaven.

*

In 1929, before Tucumcari was heaven for all those travelers, the skeleton of a 10-ton wooly mammoth was dug up just outside of town. The folks who lived there wanted to keep the skeleton, and they even built a barn-like museum to house it. But the paleontologists who were in charge of the excavation decided it needed to be in a bigger city, someplace where more people would see it, so they hauled it off to Albuquerque and reassembled it there.

Disheartened but not completely discouraged, the Tucumcari townspeople filled up their barn-like museum with other things: whale bones, a half-dozen old saddles, strands of different kinds of barbed wire, cowboy boots, gems and minerals, spear points, a windmill, a chuck wagon, several chunks of petrified wood, and a flat piece of stone they believed to be a petrified dinosaur scale. The centerpiece of the museum is an eighteen-inch piece of wooly mammoth jawbone—with two teeth intact—that some crafty fellow managed to rescue before the skeleton was taken away. They put it in a showcase with thick glass and a padlock the size of a softball.

My mother grew up in Tucumcari. Her family owned a motel there, The Weary Traveler. It had 18 rooms and a small swimming pool. When she was in high school, a senior in high school, a thin, lost-looking young man with an army green duffel bag checked in. He smiled at my mother and she fell in love with him just like that. The thin young man was, of course, my father. He stayed at their motel for four days and then left in his red car. My mother didn't see him again for more than two years but she loved him that whole time and told herself that he would come back to see her. And to see me, too, which he didn't expect.

I was a toddler by then and able to understand, partly, what my mother meant when she brought a thin, lost-looking man into my room and said, "This is your father."

Glass

I'm not going to Tucumcari alone. I'm going with my best friend, Boyd Delmarco. We have been best friends since first grade. Before the problem with his lungs started, Boyd was a well-known radio personality. He was well-known for his interesting views on things and for his wonderful voice. He still has interesting views, but his voice is all but gone, due to the problem with his lungs. He can whisper, that's about it, and even that is almost inaudible because of the oxygen mask he must wear to stay alive.

*

Boyd's lungs are turning to glass. The capillaries are crystallizing. The bronchia are turning rigid and transparent. Soon he will be as fragile as a wine goblet. If he falls, his chest will shatter. The disease that afflicts poor Boyd is called *idiopathic pulmonary fibrosis*. There is no known cure. Doctors have told Boyd the best he can hope for is two or three more active months—as active as he can be wheeling around a tank of oxygen—then he will be bedridden until air will no longer be pumped through the tubing of his lungs, and he will die.

*

Boyd's mother died because her lungs turned to glass too. It's a family problem, weak lungs. I remember his mother spending a lot of time in the kitchen, at the table, resting with one arm on the table and one in her lap. She sat like that and breathed with her whole body like a bellows, lifting and gasping. Boyd knew he was going to be the same way when he got older. He said so on his radio show and he said so when we were boys. Already, when he was just nine or ten, he could not run far without stopping to catch his breath. The other boys would run on, but I always stopped to wait.

*

In three days, on the third day, I'm going to Boyd's house, and the two of us are setting off for Tucumcari. This will be a surprise to Boyd—a real surprise!—because he doesn't know he's going with me. Boyd doesn't know he's going with me because I haven't yet told him. I won't tell him, in fact, until after I arrive at his house and have a cup of coffee and talk for a while. We'll be talking about Audrey, and he'll say in his whispery, scarred voice, "I hope I get a chance to meet her someday," and I'll say, "You will.

26

You're going to come with me," and he'll say, "I can't. I can't leave the house without these tanks, you know that," and I'll say, "We'll figure it out, just like we used to," and then he'll say, after thinking it over, "Okay, what the hell have I got to lose," and I'll say, "Not a damn thing."

*

In the days before his illness, Boyd's voice was deep and rumbling. It reminded me of a distant train. When I lived in a different city, in a different, flatter part of the country, the tracks were a mile or so from my apartment. I always knew when it was midnight because of the train that came through. You could feel the train as much as hear it, and I would fall asleep to its vibrations. Boyd's voice on the radio did the same thing for me, put me at ease.

*

Boyd's listeners, he said, fell into one of two groups: people who had never left their hometown and people who wished they had stayed.

*

When Boyd's lungs started to turn to glass and he had to give up his radio job, there was a newspaper story about him coming back to this city and moving back into his childhood home.

There was a picture, too, showing him sitting in a chair with clear tubes running from his nose to a bottle of oxygen at his feet. He was very thin, and his hair and beard were gray and sparse.

The only other picture I have of Boyd is the same one he sent out to all of his fans. In the picture, Boyd is sitting inside the studio, separated from the photographer by a wall-sized window, talking into a microphone. He looks strong in the picture, a little overweight, but vigorous. He is gesturing with both hands, and his eyes, which are fixed on nothing in particular, are wide open. His hair is bushy and black. His beard is bushy and black. He has on earphones and a shirt I am guessing is blue. He signed the picture: *Keep Your Chin Up, Boyd Delmarco.*

That was how he signed off every night, "Keep your chin up." I always liked that, keep your chin up, because it was a positive way to look at life. Or, if not positive, then hopeful. Or at least unbowed. Unbeaten.

*

The headline of the story about Boyd read: *Popular Radio Voice Falls Silent.* In the story itself, Boyd is described as "a phenomenon a decade ago whose quixotic on-air philosophizing won him a national audience." Later, it said, "Delmarco is compiling a book of the transcripts of his most popular programs. He is also working on his autobiography."

I'll be in that autobiography. When Boyd writes about his boyhood, there I'll be, at his side, arms slung across each other's shoulders and grinning. He'll tell about our escapades in the old neighborhood. He'll remember the time we thought counterfeiters were operating out of an old carriage house that sat behind the Myerly place. And, no doubt, he'll recall me being stuck up to the tops of my canvas sneakers in the middle of his grandmother's muddy garden, and how he held out a rake so I could pull myself free, only to have my shoes remain behind.

And one sock. I lost a sock, too.

*

Boyd's house is a tall, narrow house, a saltbox house. When his parents died, he inherited the place. Until he got sick and decided to come home, the house had been rented out, which means, of course, it's a little bit rundown and needs some repair. The roof probably leaks, and so does the basement. Sadly enough, Boyd can't climb the stairs back up to his boyhood bedroom where airplane models still dangle from the light fixture and pennants from college football teams are thumbtacked above his desk. The room is dusty. The wallpaper is faded, yellowed. There's a brown-edged water stain on the ceiling in the shape of Australia.

*

My old house is a squatty bungalow with a cinderblock porch across the front. I will drive past it before I go to Boyd's house and see plants hanging from the porch ceiling in front of the picture window. I will see an orange cat on the top step and a green hose lying in the yard. We had a green hose, too, I remember, but a dog instead of a cat. The dog was called Burt, named by my mother after the movie actor, Burt Lancaster. Boyd had several dogs when we were growing up. All of them were named Rusty, and all of them were hit by cars. I think they were all the same kind of dog too. Cocker spaniels.

*

Boyd lives in the house where he grew up even though a man who has threatened his life knows the address. The man's name is Osseo Fairchild and he's a real lunatic. He used to call Boyd's show every Monday night. Over the air, he would tell Boyd that he was going to kill him, so the radio station took out a million dollar life insurance policy on Boyd. Instead of being careful not to get Osseo Fairchild riled up when he called, Boyd would say things like, "Come and get me, fella," and "You know where to find me, tough guy."

*

Let me tell you some things about Osseo Fairchild.

No one knows what he looks like. No one knows where he lives.

Every time Osseo Fairchild called Boyd's program, he would chuckle when Boyd said, "You're on the air. What's on your mind?" That was how Boyd knew who it was on the other end of the line. That was how listeners knew who it was on the other end of the line. They would stop whatever they were doing and turn up the volume so that they wouldn't miss anything. The conversations would start with the topic of that night's broadcast (sexual equality, the Clear Skies Act, vandalism in rural America, dangerous chemicals) but would very quickly become threatening. Osseo Fairchild would say certain things, relate certain events in Boyd's life. They were events that only a few people would remember. "You chipped a tooth at age eleven when you were pushed into the brick façade of your elementary school by a girl who didn't want you talking to her."

Whenever Osseo Fairchild called Boyd's program, it was always from a pay phone and never in the same place twice, never in the same city twice. Once he called from a phone booth just two blocks from Boyd's studio. The police traced the call and they were there in minutes, but Osseo Fairchild had already disappeared. Boyd baited him on the air, daring him to call back, daring him to show himself. You could tell Boyd was scared but he was excited, too, hopeful. After his program went off the air that night, I was so wound up, I couldn't sleep. I spent the whole night floating near the ceiling. The next night, Boyd told us there had been a bomb in his car rigged to explode when he turned the key.

*

There was little that Boyd could do when Osseo Fairchild called but listen. More than once he said that he didn't want to take any more phone calls from him, but he told us that he was obligated by his contract to talk to anyone who called.

*

Besides Osseo Fairchild, Boyd had other regular callers to his show. Some of the people who called often were ordinary people who liked to comment on the program, but others were famous people, experts. If, for example, Boyd was talking about the weather, he would talk to a woman from Oklahoma who knew a lot about the weather, especially about tornadoes. If he wanted to tell us about laws or trees or wars or diseases, someone would call in with the answer.

*

My favorite caller was the reclusive science fiction author, C. Nash Mothpony. I am a big fan of Mothpony's books. So is Boyd. It is another thing that we have in common. Boyd was the only person Mothpony would talk to. Nobody knows what Mothpony looks like and nobody knows where he lives. He is as mysterious and elusive as Osseo Fairchild.

The last time Mothpony was on Boyd's program, he said he had just started a new book. He said it would be his greatest work and that he would probably quit writing after he finished it because everything he wanted to say would be said and none of it would have done any good in saving humanity from destroying itself.

Even though Mothpony didn't care much for people, he did care about humanity.

*

Boyd had another writer on his program, and he married her. Her name was Dolores Gray and she was a well-known mystery writer. The program she was on was about being well-known and how it can affect your life. She had just finished her fourth book, *Cruel April*, and she talked about the book as much as she talked about being well-known. She said she planned to write 12 books starring the same detective, Sylvia St. James, and each one would take place in a different month. She had already written *Jealous in January*, *Frigid February*, and *Murder in March*.

It's been a long time since she was married to Boyd, and I'm pretty sure she must have made it all the way through the calendar by now. I lost track of her after she left Boyd for a musician from Austria and moved to Salzburg. I don't even know if she's still alive. Probably she is.

*

On Friday nights, when he was still a famous radio personality, Boyd would tell his listeners to turn out their lights and, if it were possible, to look out their window at the stars. In warm weather, Boyd would sometimes broadcast from the roof of the radio station. When he couldn't go outside, he turned off the lights in the studio and rolled his chair to the window and talked about the sky. On Friday nights, with everyone looking and thinking about the stars, Boyd would tell us about the universe. He told us that 15 or 20 billion years ago there was no universe, no time and no space, just a tiny piece of very, very hot matter about the size of a proton. That's all there was anywhere. Just this proton. Then it exploded.

*

According to Irish Archbishop James Ussher, the proton exploded on the evening of October 22, 4004 B.C.

According to Polish astronomer Johannes Hevelius, it exploded on October 24, 3936 B.C., at 6 p.m.

Sir Isaac Newton said it happened in 3500 B.C., probably— even though he did not say so—at dusk on a day in late October.

*

Boyd told us, too, that very, very religious people do not believe in the proton. They believe in God, instead.

*

Some Friday nights, Boyd talked about the end of the universe. He would tell us that it would someday stop expanding and start to grow smaller and smaller until it was the size of a proton again. Then the whole thing would start over. The big explosion, etc. Many people—me included—wondered if everything would be repeated, if the earth would exist again and if each one of us would be reborn. And if we were reborn, would our lives be exactly the same or would we have a chance to do things differently?

I liked those Friday nights. I liked thinking about having a chance to do things differently. I started a list, just in case. It's a very long list, as you can imagine. Most of the things I'd change are small, everyday things. Not buying a pair of black and white checked pants I knew I would probably never wear. Not learning to dance. Not saving rare coins or stamps. Not turning down a road that looked interesting. Not telling a particular woman I loved her.

Some things, like the last one about not telling a particular woman I loved her, are big things. I don't have much hope of being able to change big things but I included some anyway, because we must always be willing to admit to great failings and feel guilt or remorse and then be willing to live in spite of them. It's hard to live that way and be happy, but I don't think we should count on being happy. What we should count on is living lives that aren't too melancholy.

In A Prior Place

Before I came to this city, I lived somewhere else, also a city but smaller than this one. It was a tourist destination, a summer destination, mostly. There were hills and lakes and woods, and the business district was designed to look like a European village. It was quaint. It had quaint shops, the kind that visitors enjoy browsing in, with candles and handmade soaps and knickknacks made out of native stone and twigs. Local artists displayed their paintings and pottery, and it was not uncommon to hear someone playing a guitar and singing on a street corner.

I worked in that city as a host at Fielder's Choice, one of a chain of restaurants owned by former professional baseball player Bobby Dart. The walls were decorated with baseball equipment and the different dining areas were named after famous ballparks: Fenway, Wrigley, Candlestick. The waiters and waitresses were all dressed like ballplayers and I was an umpire: a black jacket over an inflatable chest protector, a short-billed cap and a heavy mask that made it hard to look friendly or to be understood. Whenever someone came into the restaurant, I was to yell, "Batter up!" to let the staff know more hungry people had arrived. For kids, there was a batting cage and a pitcher's mound where they could throw balls at a bull's-eye.

It was mostly tourists who ate at Fielder's Choice, tourists with tired and cranky children who were, like their parents, red-skinned from too much sun. Sometimes, when I shouted, "Batter up!," babies would start to cry, and toddlers, angry at having been surprised, would kick my legs and bang their toes against my shin guards, making them cry, too.

*

Even if I had not read the story about Boyd and his decision to move back to his childhood home, I would not have worked at Fielder's Choice for much longer. I'm not really a baseball fan.

Once, though, shortly before I left, Bobby Dart himself showed up at the restaurant. He had been a shortstop during his playing days, so I was expecting a runt to come through the door, but he was tall with big hands and a limp. I remember he had a big head, too. I don't know how old he was. I couldn't even guess. Our manager, Dave Stevenson, who was exuberant about being our manager and wanted to be called Coach, escorted Bobby Dart around and pointed out to him things that the man had seen in every other one of his restaurants. But he acted interested and shook everyone's hand before he left, which made me think he was a pretty nice guy.

*

Most of the people who worked at Fielder's Choice were young: students from the local high school or home from college. Not all of them took the job very seriously. Those were mostly the rich kids whose families owned vacation homes on one of the lakes. They really didn't need a job at all but their parents wanted them to see what it meant to work for a living. Whenever they didn't show up for work or made the same mistake for the eighth or ninth time, Coach would bring them into his office and talk with them about being responsible. Usually, when they came out, they rolled their eyes at whoever was close by and then went back to work. No one, as far as I know, was ever fired from Fielder's Choice.

*

When I was working at Fielder's Choice, I saw the newspaper story about Boyd's being sick. Someone had left it on a table with their dirty dishes and I noticed the picture of Boyd looking peaked. The story said that Boyd had mentioned on his program that he would not be on the air much longer, but, at the time, I didn't have a radio, so I hadn't been listening for a while.

39

After work that day, I went to a department store and bought myself a new radio and was able to hear his last shows. It was sad listening to Boyd's voice getting fainter and raspier, airier. The very last night, he couldn't even make it through the whole program. He was talking to someone from a clinic in Tucumcari when his voice finally gave out. His long-time assistant, Jack Cochrane, took over and finished the interview. There was still nearly an hour left in the show, so Jack invited people to call up and say goodbye to Boyd or to share a memory with him. A lot of famous people who had been guests called in—movie stars and television personalities, musicians, scientists, writers, philosophers and religious leaders, professional athletes—and so did a lot of regular people. I thought about calling myself, but I didn't know what I would say or if I could say anything at all without choking up, so I just listened.

With six minutes to go, I heard a chuckle.

"You reap what you sow, Delmarco."

It was Osseo Fairchild.

"Just because you won't be on the radio anymore doesn't mean you're off the hook. Keep your chin up but keep looking over your shoulder, too."

Then he hung up and there was silence.

"Well," Jack Cochrane finally said, "we won't have to listen to that crackpot anymore, will we, Boyd?"

*

40

I believe that Osseo Fairchild is a master of disguise. I have no proof that's true, but it seems like it is, it seems like something a man as dangerous as Osseo Fairchild would be. I imagine him wearing false moustaches and prosthetic ears. I see him combing his hair in different styles. He goes to the same restaurant two days in a row looking completely different, just to see how effective he's been at concealing his identity. One day he is wearing a beret, another time he is in a wheelchair. There is no way of knowing with him.

*

It was because of Osseo Fairchild that I decided to go to the city where I live now to rescue Boyd. It's why I bought the station wagon, too, so that we would have room for the oxygen tanks Boyd needed. I thought I'd forgotten the reason I came here and got the car, but it turns out I didn't.

Oxygen

I think I can help Boyd live longer.

I can help him live longer if he comes with me because there is a place in the desert near Tucumcari where miraculous cures are being performed. The place is a hospital run by members of a Swiss religious order. These people use everything they can think of to get a person healthy again. They use medicine, and they use prayers, and they use vitamins, and they use machines. The kind of treatment I think will help Boyd live longer is called hyperbaric. What they will do is put him inside a huge steel cylinder filled with pure oxygen. The cylinder is pressurized so it will feel to Boyd like he is 45 feet underwater. Boyd can sit in the cylinder and read or work on his autobiography while the pure oxygen helps keep his lungs from turning to glass.

When we get there, we will be able to pick out members of the Swiss religious order helping patients be cured. You can tell which ones are the Swiss because they all wear their hair in braids, even the men.

I want to help Boyd live longer so I can talk to him, so I can listen to what he has to say. It won't be easy, I know, because his voice is ruined, but I'll be patient. I'll be quiet, and I'll listen hard.

He can talk about lots of things, anything he wants to talk about, anything under the sun. I'd like to hear more about the universe starting over again, but if Boyd doesn't want to get into that, it's fine with me. If he wants me to talk, I'll do that, too. I've got some ideas, some brainstorms, and I'd like to see what Boyd makes of them. I'd like him to see that I'm a thoughtful person, a thinker, someone who reads and thinks and ponders, which is what I do.

*

For example, here's something I read about:

Photosynthesis was invented 3.9 billion years ago by a prokaryotic cell called Promethio. Promethio was the first living being capable of taking energy from the sun and thriving on it. Promethio, of course, was named after Prometheus, who stole fire from the gods and suffered for it.

*

I think about this and then I think about the fact that if it were not for our having a molecule of zinc instead of a molecule of magnesium, we would be plants ourselves. When I think about those two things, I realize how closely we are related to lawns and flowers, and I realize that my own phototropic condition is proof.

*

I have a bottle of chlorophyll tablets and I am supposed to take them three times a day to combat my phototropic condition. The druggist warned me not to take too many or I would turn green.

Then he laughed and said he was kidding.

I knew that.

He also said that the chlorophyll tablets will make me give off small amounts of oxygen.

I knew that, too.

*

It wasn't until the end of my muddled years that my photropic condition was discovered. In fact, it was that discovery which ended that period in my life. Up until then, I had for some time been a lost cause, a sad case. But when the doctor figured out what was wrong, I became normal again. I was clear-headed. I trusted people. I had moments of joy and long stretches of contentment. I was still susceptible to floating at night (that, I was told, would never go away), but once I knew why I rose into the air the way I did, it was no longer frightening, no reason to panic.

I have other lingering effects but they're not that important.

*

Two billion years ago, almost all life on earth was wiped out by oxygen. At that time, life was microscopic and simple, just cells that survived on hydrogen. But once the hydrogen in the atmosphere was used up, and the cells started to pull it from the sea, they released oxygen. Oxygen is a powerful element. It is hungry for electrons and tears apart whatever it can sneak into to get at the electrons. It attacks everything, turning it to dust or causing it to burn up. Pretty soon, all life on earth was dying because of something it had created.

*

Boyd's problem with oxygen is that he's not getting enough into his blood because his lungs are turning to glass. Being hooked up to the tank helps but it is only a temporary solution. Before his lungs are so brittle that they won't work at all anymore, Boyd's brain will begin to starve and his thinking will go. He'll lose his memories and he'll lose his ability to do even the simplest of tasks, like feeding himself or going to the bathroom. The doctors who will treat him at the clinic near Tucumcari will help him understand all of those things and accept them. They will help me learn how to help Boyd so Audrey and I can take care of him. We will try to make his last days pleasant. We will try to make him as happy as we can.

*

The first living being that learned to deal with oxygen and proliferate was called Prospero. It was named after the character in Shakespeare's play, *Tempest*. In that play, Prospero had to use magic against the characters who wanted to destroy him.

*

Oxygen is still one of the most destructive elements on earth. It destroys through a process called oxidation. Rust is a form of oxidation. So is fire.

For something to catch fire and burn, there must be three factors present. There must be a combustible material. There must be heat. And there must be oxygen.

*

The newspaper story about Boyd said he has to buy the oxygen he breathes from a company that specializes in respiratory equipment and prosthetic devices. The oxygen comes in silver cylinders about two feet long that fit into a cart Boyd can push or drag along when he walks. Each cylinder holds two hours of oxygen. When the company brings Boyd his oxygen, they bring him six days' worth, which means six plastic crates with a dozen cylinders in each crate. They take the empties back and fill them up again.

We won't be able to do this once we're on the road to Tucumcari. We'll have to think of something else.

*

When Boyd and I are on the road heading for Tucumcari, we'll have adventures. Some of these adventures will be momentous. Others will be mildly pleasant or strangely familiar or a little irritating. That's how adventures go. That's how it is when you're on the road. Nothing is planned. All meetings are accidental. Coincidence and chance decide everything.

*

Once when I was traveling, I met a man who owned a dead whale. He had the whale in a semi-truck trailer filled with water. One side of the trailer was glass so people who paid fifty cents could look in at the dead whale floating there. The glass was covered with a canvas flap the man kept tied down as he drove from town to town so people couldn't get a free look. A picture of a whale was painted on the canvas to advertise what was inside the trailer. That whale looked alive, though. It had water shooting out of its blowhole and it was smiling.

47

The man told me he'd been showing the whale for eight years at county fairs and schools. He said there was no better life in the world.

Another time, I met a brother and a sister who were trying to find and photograph all of their living relatives.

Another time, I drove through a town that had burned to the ground.

Another time, I met Audrey.

Saturday

Once, last winter, I saw a woman who reminded me of Audrey. This was before I remembered Audrey, so it's probably more accurate to say the woman I saw reminded me of someone who turned out to be Audrey.

*

It was a Saturday morning when I saw her, cold and gray and snowy. Or maybe it wasn't snowy, maybe the ash was especially heavy that day. But I know it was a Saturday morning because that's when most of the men who live in my neighborhood are out. The sidewalks are thick with us, our heads bent over lists of things to do or things to buy, lists written on the back of last week's grocery receipt. We duck in and out of the stores. We go in to drop off dry cleaning. We go in to buy new shoes or a pack of cigarettes. The stores are so full of us that sometimes doors won't close, and we have to wait outside.

Surprisingly, there are very few pedestrian collisions on

these congested mornings. Brushed shoulders are common, but a skull-knocking, staggering and reeling kind of crack-up rarely happens. It's more likely that a taxi or a delivery van will clip a daydreamer and send him cartwheeling down the street.

The Saturday I saw the woman who reminded me of Audrey, I was feeling buoyant. No, that's not quite right. I was feeling a little weightless, a little less pulled at by gravity, which happens when it's overcast, which was the case that morning. It was very overcast, very gray with clouds that were so low and thick I could have reached up and patted them.

I was one of the shoppers that morning, one of the men in galoshes tromping through gray slop. The reason I went out that morning was my galoshes. I had bought them at a place that sold all sorts of rugged clothing and garden tools and parts for small engines, but they turned out to be faulty. One of the buckles was sprung or twisted. I couldn't tell which, but it didn't close tightly, and my foot got wet every time I went out. In fact, it was getting wet that morning on my way to the store, which made me peevish and gave me peevish ideas about what I would say to the clerk who had sold them to me.

"I'd like my money back, please."

"I expect you to refund my money or give me a new pair."

"Do you realize how uncomfortable this is?"

"Look at this. My shoes are ruined."

I was tramping past the butcher shop when I saw the woman who reminded me of Audrey. She was in the butcher shop. She was working there. I saw her come out from a back room and put a tray of something into one of the big glass cases that held coiled sausages and great slabs of bloody meat. Her hair was braided in a long, thick rope that hung to her waist. I think it hung to her waist. The place was crowded with men in dark topcoats, and the glass case cut her off from my view just below the shoulders, so I could only see that much of her, the top part, but I thought I knew her from somewhere and thought I remembered her hair as well.

By the time I had squeezed myself into the store, the woman who looked like Audrey had retreated into the back room again and the door had swung shut behind her, so all I got was that glimpse of her red hair, a bit of her profile. The whole time I was making my way closer and closer to the counter, I waited for her to return. I thought about asking the butcher who she was but when I finally got to the counter, all I could do was ask him for a pound of stew meat. Back on the street, I looked through the window just as the butcher pushed open the door and I caught a second, quick glimpse of red hair. That was all.

I went back the next Saturday and the one after that, but she wasn't there either time. I would have gone back again but by then I had enough stew meat to last me for months.

*

Sometimes, when I think of Audrey, I think it may be the only memory I have. I think that I am always remembering her, that somewhere on the edge of every other thought that passes through my brain, she is there.

This is what I believe it's like to be in love with someone.

Needle, Haystack

Since Boyd moved back to this city, back into his boyhood home, I have begun to look for Osseo Fairchild because I know that he is here in this city, too. He is here in this city and he is here in this neighborhood. I know this because this neighborhood is the perfect place to go unnoticed, to be seen and not seen. Probably I have passed him many times, bumped shoulders, shrugged an apology and missed the smile, the knowing, sly smile of a man intent on doing no good. I try to remember those occasions, note the downward glance, the dangling cigarette, turned-up collar, cocked hat. I am as vigilant as a hawk hovering above a stripped cornfield. I see him everywhere. I see him nowhere. Who am I looking for? How will I know him? I think of ways to draw him out, expose him. I stand on crowded corners and shout his name to see who turns but he is too clever for that, too clever to look. But he might flinch or duck his head and try to disappear in the crush of men in overcoats and dark fedoras. That's what I need to stay alert for, what I need to be able to spot: his being there and then not, his vanishing.

53

I remember when I realized I could make myself vanish. I think it's my first memory. It was when my mother and I lived in an apartment behind the check-in desk at The Weary Traveler. This was before my father came to take us with him. What I remember is standing between two mirrors, in the narrow space between two mirrors that ran from floor to ceiling next to the counter where people checked in. If I stood very still with my back pressed against the wall, when people came into the lobby they would look at themselves in the mirror but they would never see me. They would wipe sweat off their faces or check their teeth or hair but I went unseen. Sometimes, a man and a woman would come in together and they would not be able to keep their hands off each other. If it took my mother a minute or two to come to the counter after the man had slapped his hand on the bell, they would grab and touch each other in a way that seemed too private for a motel lobby, even to me, young as I was, small as I was.

Once when my mother came out, she smiled at the couple, who had smoothed their clothes and arranged themselves generally, and then she saw me standing between the mirrors. I was never invisible to her. She told me to go to our apartment, to wait for her. The two people turned and were surprised when I emerged from the mirrors, and it dawned on them that I had watched their shenanigans. The woman's face turned red and she put her hand to her cheek, but the man smiled and rubbed the top of my head with his knuckles, not hard enough to hurt.

Ever since then, ever since I realized I could become invisible, I have seen other people who had discovered the same thing. One man I can see from my apartment window always wears gray and, while he waits for the bus, he stands with his back against the stone building next to the bus stop and fades away. I watched another man once in a different place, a different city, who walked in the shadows of other people on the sidewalk, his body bending and stretching to fit the different shapes. I remember him because he saw me see him and was startled. He lost his concentration and came out into the bright light and was staggered by it.

*

There are probably many reasons why people choose to be invisible. Maybe they're shy or afraid, maybe they did something wrong and are humiliated or hunted. Maybe they wish to stay invisible to keep an eye on someone. Maybe keep an eye on everyone.

*

When I lived with my mother in the Weary Traveler and discovered I could make myself invisible, motels were low, flat places, usually shaped like an L or a U. Some had swimming pools. Some had diners. At all of them, you pulled your car right up to the door of the room that you rented, which made it easy to unpack your car. And to keep an eye on it, too.

That's what I want to find when I'm traveling with Boyd, a motel like that where I can keep an eye on the car and the parking lot. While Boyd sleeps and his air tank hisses, I'll sit next to the window with the curtain pulled back just enough and make sure we're safe.

You Must Remember This

I read somewhere that we live 80% of our lives in our heads. That seems reasonable. A reasonable percentage, 80. For some people, it's higher, I'm sure. People who are quadriplegic, for example, or people whose muscles are destroyed by disease would live almost all of their lives in their heads. So would people without any limbs at all. But there are other people, too, who have a higher percentage by choice. Boyd is one of those people, one of those who lives in his head a lot more than most.

Boyd lives in his head because he is always remembering how things used to be, how life used to be. When he was on the radio, he would talk about what he remembered. He would tell stories. Some of the stories, like those involving me, would be stories from his own life, his own history. He would also tell us about history in a bigger way, the history of a place or an event. He did not remember all of those, of course, because some of them happened before he was alive, but telling us about them made us remember so we wouldn't forget how important certain places or events were. Some nights, if there were listeners who had been alive when the story Boyd was telling happened, they might call in to reminisce or to add something to the story.

*

Once, when Boyd was recalling the Dust Bowl years, a woman who had grown up in South Dakota called with her recollection of the grasshoppers that plagued the land. She said she was just a small girl standing in front of the farmhouse where she lived with her parents and two sisters when the sun was blocked out by a cloud of whirring spring-legged insects that dropped out of the sky—millions and millions of them—and they ate the already drought-stunted corn and beans and oats and wheat right down to the dry, cracked ground. Then they rose up and blew away, rising and falling from one field to the next. The woman remembered in particular how the grasshoppers had frightened their plow horses, a pair of matched black horses, who took off at a dead run and could not be found for days. When her father finally located them, they were standing in a creek with dozens of other horses, all of them caked in mud they had rolled in to protect themselves from the swarm. She started to tell about the pastor at their church, who used the incident to scare everyone into thinking sin had caused the infestation, but Boyd told her he had to move on to the next caller.

I liked the woman's story. It was very descriptive and had emotion, and I imagined what it would have been like to be there that day, what it would have been like to be in the middle of the cloud of grasshoppers, to hear the rattle of all those wings, to feel them hit my face and land on my arms.

Most of my own life, when I remember it, seems imagined, too, as real as this one, as real as that one.

*

I can't trace back through my life like some people can, going back as if they were walking a path that leads straight into the past, remembering that this followed this, which came before this, and so on. My life is more like a photo album someone dropped and all the pictures fell out. Whoever put them back in didn't pay any attention to the order, so now I remember, say, a day in school—sixth grade—when a jar of dead frogs broke and the room filled with the strange smell of formaldehyde, and then, for no reason clear to me, I remember a time I found someone's wallet and kept the money.

*

Photos are not a good way to think of memories, not a good comparison. A guest on Boyd's show said that people have the wrong idea about how we remember. "A memory is not an object," he said, "It's not a book you can pull off a shelf and open to a particular page you marked some time earlier." The man was a brain scientist from England and he was talking to Boyd over the telephone from London. He told Boyd and those of us listening that you can't retrieve a memory that is the same as it was the last time because you are not the person now that you were the last time you remembered whatever it was that you were remembering or think you remembered. The important things are still there, that's why it's stuck in your brain anyway, but it might not mean the same thing because other things have happened to you, and all of those things together make up a new memory, a new story, which is part of the bigger story of your life.

The brain scientist also said that you can project yourself into the future because you can remember what has gone on before and use those memories to imagine what is yet to come based on those experiences. He said your ability to do this keeps you from being surprised by things that will happen. You won't know what will occur exactly, but you will have had similar instances that let you recognize and understand what's happening. It's why people don't step out in front of a bus, he said, or try to pet a snarling dog.

Some people, he said, have a problem in their brains that makes them think in the future all of the time. He said they live in a constant state of déjà vu. Everything they do they believe they have done before. He called this "the feeling of remembering" and said that nothing could be done to help the people who had the condition. Their whole life would be a memory before it had ever even happened.

About My Mother and Her Stories

My mother used to write stories and send them to magazines to be published. Her stories were very short, and the magazines always sent them back to her and told her that she needed to flesh things out more, make her characters more fully realized, construct a plot.

She kept all of the stories and she kept all of the letters from the magazines telling her what she should do. I have all of it, the stories and the letters.

My mother would write her stories on a little gray typewriter that she kept on the kitchen table. My father would complain about having to eat with the typewriter next to him but she refused to move it.

"And be careful you don't spill on my pages," she would add.

After she wrote her stories, my mother would read them to my father and me.

"This is a true story," she would say.

Whenever she told me something about her own life or that she had heard from someone else, she always started with "This is a true story." To her, being a true story was very important, even if it wasn't true.

Here is one of her stories. It's one of my favorites:

Each night, a star falls from the sky in the west, over the mountains. The round-faced boy has watched them fall every night. He cannot sleep—he's never been able to sleep—once the sun goes down. Something he cannot name stirs inside him after dark and he stands at the window of his room, watching the sky. He stands there until he sees the star fall, then he turns on the radio, very softly, and listens to the Word of God.

The man who speaks the Word of God is across town in a corrugated tin building beneath a tall tower. It is hot in the tin building. The generator that carries the man's voice out into the night, into the desert all the way to the mountains, a huge diesel-driven generator chuffing black smoke, is a furnace that fires the Word, hardens it into truth pure as a diamond, but it is killing the man, cooking him slowly. He has lost all of his hair and his skin is blistered.

Still, he comes in at dusk, starts the generator, closes the door and opens the Bible at the spot where he had left off just before sunrise when the fuel in the engine was spent, and the great machine coughed and popped, then squealed to a halt. Since he began many years earlier, the man has read every word, from Genesis to The Book of Revelation, more than thirty times. There are entire chapters he can recite without looking, with his eyes closed and his lips grazing the chrome screen of the microphone. When he does this, through the headset, his own voice is unfamiliar, and he wonders what it will be like when he will no longer need to look at any page. He won't even need to open the book. Perhaps, he tells himself, his body will have burned away by then, leaving only his voice.

*

After my mother read this story to my father and me, I asked her if the boy who listened to the radio was a boy like me, if I was like the boy in the story.

"I don't know," she said. "What do you think?"

*

My mother liked to rewrite her stories after she received the letters from the magazines offering her advice. Instead of listening to their suggestions about making her stories longer, she made them shorter. The story about the round-faced boy, for example, kept going the first time she wrote it:

It is dawn, and the man who reads the Bible on the radio all night is ready to go home. He puts on a pair of sunglasses and goes out to his car. It is important that he get home before the sun is up completely because he cannot stand the light. In the sun, his raw skin crackles. He must be in a dark place, an air-conditioned place where he can sleep with an ice pack on his chest.

Before he goes to sleep, he reads his mail. He is surprised to find a letter among the flyers and bills. It is a letter addressed to him in a child's handwriting. It is a letter from a boy who listens to him every night after watching for shooting stars. The man is touched by the boy's kind words. He decides to write back and does, thanking the boy for listening and reminding him that the words he hears are the words of truth. He reminds the boy to live by those words and not to be tempted. "If there is anything I can ever do to make your life better," the man writes, "just let me know," and he means it.

After he falls asleep, the man dreams of shooting stars. He dreams he is standing in the desert and the whole sky is streaked with them.

Some stories she pared down to a single paragraph and one became a single sentence, six lines on a sheet of white paper:

When, in her mind, she traveled beyond the walls of her house, beyond the fence that ran along the road, beyond the fields and the towns, the cities, the oceans, mountains, forests, deserts, she always found herself arriving at her own back door.

*

I am rewriting my mother's stories. In the morning, with my first cup of coffee, I sit at her old typewriter, roll in a piece of clean paper and get to work. I am almost finished. When I rewrite the last one, I will send them to a publisher, along with a letter explaining that these stories are my mother's way of making sense of the world. I will explain that they all take place in the same town, Tucumcari, where she grew up, and that all of them are true.

The young woman washes dishes at the kitchen sink and looks out the window at the desert, the mountains, the sky. She does this every day, and every day the view is the same. After a while, because nothing changes, she begins to lose track of time. She is not sure what day it is, what month, what year. She looks at her hands, red from the hot soapy water, and sees the hands of an old woman, the hands of a child. One day, after centuries have passed in her mind, she sees something different, something out of the ordinary, moving across the flat desert floor. It is a plume of dust, a dervish, swirling and swaying. As she watches, the column grows larger, taller and thicker, darker with the sand it pulls up into itself. She can see its shadow like a finger pointing in her direction. She dries her hands and waits for it to arrive.

A Match Made In Heaven

Before I met my father, before he showed up at The Weary Traveler, my mother would tell me stories about him, about how the two of them met and fell in love. Like all of my mother's stories, she said that these were true, too.

*

My mother and my father were childhood sweethearts, two kids from the sand hills of Nebraska who had always expected to marry each other. My father worked on a cattle ranch, riding horses and branding calves. He wore a straw cowboy hat in the summer and a felt hat in the winter. My mother's father owned the ranch. He liked my father and was happy the two of them were going to be married.

When the war came along and split them up for a few years, a few long years, my mother's father—my grandfather—told my father everything would be just the same when he came back as it was when he left. He said it would be like no time had passed at all.

My father and my mother were older when they met and married. It was after the war a few years and he was selling textbooks and she was an elementary school teacher. Neither of them ever expected to get married.

But, then, neither of them expected to meet the other, either.

*

My father and my mother were introduced by a mutual friend at a dance, and by the end of the evening knew they would someday be married. This took place in Pennsylvania, where my mother was a nurse in a veterans' hospital, and my father was repairing typewriters and vacuum cleaners. The dance took place in a hotel called the Rembrandt, in a ballroom with chandeliers and velvet wall hangings.

*

My father and my mother met at a motel and , after a while, got married, and the three of us lived in many places, most of them safe from atomic bombs.

Nuclear Family

Someday I will write a book about my father because he helped build the first atomic bomb.

*

My father helped build the first atomic bomb, but he wasn't one of those famous men whose names you always read in books about the bomb. He was just a soldier in the army sent out into the desert. He didn't know what was going on before he got there, and when he did get there, he found out the big shots didn't really know what was going on, either, except that they were trying to create the most destructive weapon the world had ever seen, and they weren't sure they could do it, and they weren't sure what it would do if they did. Some of them speculated that it might evaporate the atmosphere. Some others thought it might crack the earth's crust and send tectonic plates skidding around and banging into each other like shuffleboard pucks. But that didn't stop them from going ahead with their project.

70

"It was like a bunch of boys poking with sticks at a rattlesnake," my father said. "They knew if they poked enough, it would strike. They just had to be ready to run."

*

When the bomb went off, it was brighter than 20 suns. The heat was the same as the sun's core, and it turned the sand into glass. My father took a chunk of the melted sand. It was about the size of a quarter and looked like the greenish glass soft drink bottles are sometimes made from. *Atomsite* is what they called the stuff, that or *trinitite*. I still have the piece my father chipped free. It's in the same box as my father's medals from the army and my mother's stories, the same box as my parents' ashes.

*

When the bomb went off, my father was standing next to the famous genius Enrico Fermi. During the countdown, Enrico Fermi tore up some paper into little bits. As soon as he felt the blast wave from the bomb, he dropped the paper. After the wave passed, he measured how far the paper had been blown by the blast wave, and then he used his slide rule to figure out how many tons of TNT it would take to do what the bomb had done. My father was the one who handed Enrico Fermi his slide rule when the famous scientist dropped it because his hands were shaking.

My father was the one he turned to and said, "20,000 tons." My father was the one who whispered, "Jesus Christ."

*

When the bomb went off, Robert Oppenheimer, who was also a famous genius, turned to someone, not my father, and said, "I am become Death, the destroyer of worlds."

I don't know if the person he said that to had anything to say in reply.

*

I've read a lot over the years about the first atomic bomb. I probably know more about it than anything else I can think of.

I know that after the first bomb exploded, a soldier at the site turned on a faucet in his barracks, and worms came out with the water.

I know that there was a cat that became famous because its black fur was speckled white from the fallout.

I know there was a girl who could see the flash even though she was blind.

*

The first atomic bomb didn't even look like a bomb. It looked like a wrecking ball, which it was.

The second atomic bomb flattened Hiroshima.

To make an atomic bomb, you need two pieces of uranium each a little bigger than half the critical size needed for a successful chain reaction. These two pieces of uranium have to be kept apart until you want the chain reaction to begin. When it's time for that to happen, you bring the two pieces together very rapidly. Usually, one of the pieces is shot at the other one, like a bullet. When they hit, the atoms split apart, sending neutrons flying at thousands of miles per hour. These neutrons split more atoms, which split more and more and more. All of this happens in a millionth of a second, not even enough time to blink your eyes, and what you have is a tremendous amount of energy being released in the form of a nuclear explosion. Here's what happens when those atoms start flying:

If the bomb is dropped directly over a city, 200 square blocks will be flattened, and thousands of people will be incinerated. A half-mile wide crater will be left behind.

At one mile from the site of the explosion, the air will be hotter than 50 suns, and the blast wave will knock over walls nine inches thick.

At two miles, wood will char instantly. So will skin.

At two-and-a-half miles, billboards will be knocked over.

At up to ten miles, there will be fires. Gas lines will be ruptured and electric lines knocked down by the thermal wind.

Flying glass will be a danger.

All of this will take place in less than one minute.

*

The bomb is a metaphor for man's greatest fear. Mankind always had metaphors for that fear, but it was usually some kind of monster or some kind of cataclysmic act of God. We are the first to have created the very thing we fear the most.

*

The book I'm going to write, a book about the first atomic bomb, will be called *The One Who Whispered*, and it will be about the part my father played. It will go beyond that, too. It will go right up to his death, which means I'll be in the book. I'll be able to tell about how my father used to blow things up when he was a boy. He told me about that many times. He told me that he and his best friend would make bombs out of firecrackers and soup cans. My father's best friend lost an eye making bombs but the love of things exploding was too great for my father to give it up because of an accident.

"It's energy in its most basic form," he would say to me. "You think you can control it, but you can't. Not the way you want it to, anyway."

He would tell me this while we were constructing little

74

bombs of our own, the two of us in the basement or in the garage. Sometimes we used gunpowder and sometimes we mixed different chemicals together. Most of the time, we just blew holes in the ground but once we knocked a dead limb off a tree. My father was going to cut it down before it fell and hurt someone, then he decided it would be more interesting and less work to blast it off. When it hit the ground, it was on fire. We let it burn and then picked up the charred chunks and threw them away.

"You can do this to people, too, you know." He held a piece of blackened wood in his hand. "I've seen it done."

This was before I learned about his part in building the first atomic bomb and before we started moving around because my father was having nervous breakdowns and couldn't keep a job. That was when we owned the station wagon, the one I remember.

In the book, I'll tell about growing up after I found out about my father and the atomic bomb. I'll tell about how I knew what my father had done but couldn't say anything because everyone was so afraid of nuclear war that I didn't think anyone would see his actions as particularly heroic or praiseworthy. Nobody at that time thought having the bomb was a good idea, except for the generals and the president, and they weren't all that sure themselves. My father couldn't tell anyone, either, about his part in building the bomb. All anyone knew about him was that he sold encyclopedias or he was a shoe clerk or that he opened the new soft-serve ice cream place on the edge of town. When we lived in this city, he was trying his hand at managing a tool and die shop. He didn't run any equipment, he just made sure other people ran it the right way and didn't get hurt.

*

I think about my father at this time of day, sunset, when the falling ash turns red. The clouds of ash turn red too and the whole world outside my window seems to have caught fire. I think about my father then because I think that this might have been what the whole world looked like to him when the bomb went off.

My father finally died of cancer. The bomb got him, too.

*

The clouds are getting darker, blackening. I can no longer see ash in the air.

It is night, and I am still here.

It is night, and I start to float.

I will spend the night floating.

A man in ragged, roomy clothes drags a child's wagon down a narrow street. In this part of the city, all of the streets are narrow, all of the buildings are falling down. The wagon's wheels squeak as they cut through the dust like a sled's runners cut into snow. Their track wavers, weaves from curb to curb, following the man as he makes his way toward the boarded-up filling station where he sleeps. The wheels squeak but no one—save the man—hears them turn. No one lives here except him and no one comes here anymore. In the purple light of late afternoon, he pulls his empty, screeching wagon and talks to himself.

The man was a soldier once, stationed in the desert where atomic bombs were detonated. He was ordered to watch and was given goggles with smoked lenses to protect his eyes. He stood at attention in his special goggles and his uniform while the great mushroom cloud rose higher and unbelievably higher and sand driven by the bomb's hot wind scoured the skin from his hands and face. His skin now is red and leathery, pocked with bleeding sores, and his eyes see only shadows.

Every day the man pulls his wagon through deserted streets to that part of Tucumcari where restaurants and nightclubs line the busy highway. He travels the alleys behind the restaurants and nightclubs, searching through the garbage bins for food. The busboys stepping out for a smoke call him over, give him a sandwich, ask him to tell them again about the bomb. In a voice burned to a whisper, he remembers for them the fiery billow, makes them feel the heat, helps them to see there in the boiling, spreading cloud what he saw: the figure of Christ crucified rising toward heaven, pulling his hands and feet free of the nails that have held him for centuries, come back to earth, unleashed by science, to judge the living and the dead.

Under the Weather

A morning like this makes me forget I can float. Gravity and the weight of air, the weight of light, pin me down. My head is deep in the pillow and cannot be raised. Every time my heart beats, I can feel the blood move in my skull. I feel sick. I can taste stomach acid.

And it's raining.

Another day I might like the sound of rain hitting my window, the smell of it, the purity of air cleaned of ash. I might feel soothed. But today, drops fall like broken glass, all jangle.

I have a terrible headache and bile in my throat. My leg is twisted in the sheets. My arm is asleep. I can't move. I don't want to move. My eyes won't open, but I know the light is gray, and I can feel that the air is cold and damp.

*

I was awakened before dawn this morning, which may have contributed to my feeling so leaden, so anchored. I was

79

awakened by a sound from the street. I could hear it clearly even though my window was closed. I could hear a sound like a book being dropped and then a grunt followed by the same: dropped book, grunt. I got up and pulled back my curtain just enough and could see two men in the street below. They were dressed similarly in top coats and fedoras, and each carried a briefcase. It was the briefcases that made the sound I thought was a dropped book. It made the sound when one of the men would swing his briefcase back and then forward, catching the other man in the shoulder or back or chest, depending on his position. The man who was struck would grunt and then swing his briefcase and hit the other one in the shoulder or back or chest. They did this again and again, back and forth, hitting and grunting. Around their feet, a cloud of ash swirled. They did not speak to each and they did not, either of them, seem to be getting tired.

I looked up and down the street and I looked at the windows of the apartments opposite my own to see if anyone else had heard the two men, if anyone else was watching. But I saw no sign, no curtain moving or blind slat pulled down. I let my curtain drop and crawled back into bed, already feeling ill, and lay there listening. I didn't think I would be able to get back to sleep, but when I opened my eyes again, the sun was up, and the only sound outside was the scrape of snow shovels.

*

Sometimes the air in this city gets so thick with ash and dust that people get sick, and some people die. On days like that, sirens are blown to warn everyone to stay inside. The police cruise the streets looking for people who did not hear the warnings or ignored them. This is one of those days. I think it was the siren that woke me up, but I don't recall hearing it, and now I think I can hear a voice on a loud speaker

When I get to Tucumcari, I won't have to feel this way anymore. I won't float anymore. I won't need to explain myself.

*

On nice days, days when the ash is blown away by the wind and the sun appears, I walk to the park next to the river and watch ducks. I used to bring along stale bread and feed the ducks, but that usually resulted in their becoming unreasonable, so now I just keep an eye on them but don't let them know I see everything they do. Ducks can tell you a lot about what might happen, which is why I watch them.

*

It was my father who taught me that birds were more than feathers and beak. He had a great affinity for birds. I think he would much rather have been a bird, the flying away, the view. Sometimes he would stop the car and get out to listen to a meadowlark on a fence post. In the fall, when the birds began to gather for their trip south, he would stand under them as hundreds of them flew overhead, looping and stretching, changing direction, one minute a ball, the next a snake.

"They're starlings," he said to me. "It's how they fool hawks into thinking they're all one big bird."

My father also had a record of bird sounds, bird songs. Evenings after he got home from work, he would get out the record, put it on the player and then practice whistling like the different species. After he did one side, he would flip the record over, take a sip of water and clear his throat, and then do the second side. When he finished, my mother would offer her opinion.

"The mourning dove was a little nasal tonight," she might say. Or, "That was a wonderful cardinal."

At some point, the record got broken. My father talked about buying another one, but the record player we had was old and the needle all but shot, so he didn't bother. He still whistled, though, as many of the songs as he could remember. When his cancer got bad, it got too hard for him and he stopped trying to talk with the birds and just studied them instead. He filled a notebook with his observations. I still have it. It's a blue spiral notebook with the words "What Birds Mean" written on the front. It's not completely full, but there are many pages of notes that my father included. Here are a few examples:

Two swallows swooping in tandem: delight or, in the morning with rain pending, anxiety

Hawk: gliding: good luck; on the ground or in a tree: be vigilant!!

Snowy Egret: patience, unless in proximity to a Great Blue Heron, then resolve whatever is on your mind

Killdeer: on the ground, tender feelings; in flight: a good time to call an old friend.

*

Where I live now, here in this city, the only birds I see are pigeons. They are everywhere. But they don't mean anything, nothing at all. My father told me that pigeons have spent so much time around people that they have lost their ability to have mystery or meaning. He said they are just little feathered people who go about their daily business, skittering to get out of the way when something happens that they didn't expect.

*

When I was a boy and felt like this, sick like this, my mother would let me stay home from school. She would let me stay home but she also made me stay in bed. She wanted to make sure I understood that being sick meant more than staying home from school. It meant you couldn't do anything but malinger. When I had the mumps, though, and was in bed for five days, my mother bought me a word puzzle book, which I finished by the time I felt better and only had to look at the answers in the back a few times.

I will stay in bed today but I don't have a word puzzle book.

I will stay in bed and listen to the rain instead. I will listen to it pound against my window and try to make it sound soothing.

I will stay in bed until it's time to get up to teach my students.

I will stay in bed and think about something else, maybe birds.

Civil Defense

Because my father helped build the atomic bomb and because he had seen what it could do, he was always careful about where he took us to live. Anything that might attract an atomic bomb, like military bases or factories where they made planes or tanks, was avoided.

At one time my father talked about getting a trailer to pull behind the car so we'd always be ready to go, to find a safe place, when the sirens went off. He even brought home a brochure describing the features of one of these trailers. It wasn't the sleek silver ones that look like they belong on the highway. It was more like a corrugated box on wheels, white with a wide aqua stripe that ran around the whole thing just below the windows. Inside, it was paneled with dark wood or something like wood, something that looked like wood, and it had furniture like the furniture you find in a motel room. My father wanted the trailer and he talked about it for months. But my mother didn't want to live in a tin can. That's what she said, that's how she described it: a tin can. So my father

85

threw away the brochure. Even more than being safe, he wanted my mother to be happy.

The only time we lived in a risky place was when we moved here, to this city. By that time, my father was sick and needed to be close to a hospital where they could treat him. After it became clear that it was hopeless and my father was going to die no matter what, we went to California so he could see what it was like living near an ocean for a while. He wanted to go on up to Alaska and see what it was like living on a glacier, but he got too weak and had trouble even getting out of bed. The last place he lived was a little white house on a cliff looking down on the Pacific Ocean.

He liked it there.

We all liked it there.

*

My father got his information about safe places to live from a civil defense manual he received from the government. The manual was titled *Personal and Family Survival*, and it had maps that showed strategic targets and where fallout would drift because of prevailing winds.

According to the maps, one of the safest places to live was Tucumcari.

*

When the war ended, my father had no idea what he would do with his life so he stayed in the army. He didn't have anything to do with the bomb anymore, but it stuck with him, the cloud, the heat and the light, what it could do. The army tried to help him forget. When he complained about nightmares and insomnia, they prescribed medicine that was supposed to get rid of anxiety and worry. When he couldn't handle the duties he was assigned, they gave him something else to do. Every time they gave him a new job, they gave him an easier one, something they thought he could do that wouldn't trigger his anxiety and worry. The last job he got was filling truck tires with air. One day, in another part of the huge garage where he was working, someone put too much air into a tire and it exploded. A piece of rubber, black and about the size of a half-dollar, flew across the room and hit him on the cheek.

While others were running toward the man who had overinflated the tire and now lay on the floor, covering his face with his hands and screaming, my father dropped his air hose and headed in the opposite direction. He walked across the base to the barracks and packed his duffel bag. At the gate to the base, a sentry stopped him and asked him what he was doing.

"I think I'll go now," my father said. "I think I've been a soldier long enough."

No one disagreed with him and though they wouldn't let him leave that day, the next week he was given a medical discharge and a bus ticket, which he never used. Instead, he bought a red car and drove west. He drove back to the desert to the place where the bomb went off. He went to ground zero. There wasn't much to see: some twisted pieces of rusty steel. The sand was melted. It had turned into green glass. He broke off a piece of the green glass and put it in his shirt pocket. Then he got back into his car and drove and drove and drove. He really never stopped driving. His whole life, he never stopped moving.

*

Because my father helped build the first atomic bomb, it was up to me to warn my classmates about radiation burns and fallout and bomb shelters. But I was usually new to a school and not very outgoing, so the only chance I had to tell them what I knew, what I had learned from my father's civil defense manual, was when I had to get up in front of everybody and give a report. Even if we were supposed to be talking about a book we had read or about a science experiment we were going to try, I talked about the atomic bomb instead.

*

The civil defense manual had directions for building a bomb shelter and told what supplies you would need to survive for two weeks. At the end of two weeks, you could come out to see if anyone else was still alive. Then you were supposed to go to the post office and fill out a survivor registration form, called a Safety Notification Card, and send it to Washington, D.C. so the government would know who was alive and where they were. If you couldn't live in your home anymore, you were supposed to fill out an Emergency Change of Address card and mail that as well.

The manual didn't say what you were supposed to do if the post office was gone.

*

Not everyone could afford to build a real bomb shelter, of course, so the manual had low-cost alternatives to the underground structures that were outfitted with steel doors and air filtration systems and bunk beds. The alternatives were more like kids' forts, the kind where you would put a blanket over a card table or kitchen chairs. The shelters were cubbyholes under piles of furniture and luggage and anything else you could throw on to soak up the radiation. If you had a basement, you could build your shelter down there and, for added protection, fill the bathtub on the first floor with water. If you didn't have a basement, you could make a shelter in just about any room so long as you boarded up the windows. There was even a design for a lean-to against the outside of your house.

None of the houses we lived in had a bomb shelter because

my father didn't believe in them. He knew enough about radiation to know you were never really safe from it and sitting around in a hole or under a sofa wasn't going to do much to save your life. His plan, besides trying to avoid places where bombs might be dropped, was to be ready to outrun the radiation. With the map that showed where fallout would drift after the bomb went off, he figured we should be ready to take off at a moment's notice. Which is why we had boxes we never unpacked and why we never bought any furniture. Everything we owned could be put into our station wagon.

That's true now, too. Everything I own will fit into my station wagon, with plenty of room left over.

*

My father never once doubted that there would be an atomic war. Having been with the scientists and soldiers who put together the first bomb and watching them and listening to them, he was certain they would find a reason to drop another one. That's one of the reasons we moved so much. That and his nervous breakdowns, which were caused by his worrying about the bomb being dropped and his helping to build it in the first place.

*

For six years, the United States kept a bomber carrying an

atomic bomb in the air over West Germany. There were actually four of these bombers carrying A-bombs, and they took turns taking off, flying around in big circles for six hours and then landing. All of the crews on the four bombers knew that if the Russians attacked, they would be headed toward Moscow to blow it up.

I don't know if that's exactly right, if that's exactly what they did, but I do know that there are still 11 unexploded atomic bombs lying in places around the world where they don't belong. One of them is stuck in the mud at the mouth of the Savannah River in Georgia, and two more are on the ocean floor off the coast of New Jersey. In West Germany, a bomb was accidentally dropped over a small village. It ended up half-buried in the main street where it still remains. Removing it is more dangerous than leaving it, but the people who must live with it in the middle of their village in the middle of their main street move around it very carefully and quietly. No cars or trucks are allowed in the village, and there can be no parades or loud music. Most people suffer from nightmares or insomnia, and the children are stunted in their growth and are very timid.

*

After the war and after I was born, my father started writing letters to politicians. In the letters, he would tell them that he had been a soldier but had never been in combat, never shot anybody, never stabbed anybody or attacked anybody with his bare hands. But, he told them, "I helped kill thousands of people, and I have a hard time sleeping because of it."

With Some Frequency

We had a portable radio that my father always had tuned to 640 or 1240, which were the two AM frequencies designated by the government as the civil defense warning system. In case of an atomic war, every radio station in the country was supposed to change its frequency to one of those two so that the government could reach everyone with important news about how to survive the bombs and missiles heading our way.

There were two red triangles on the radio dial that made it easy to find the stations that would tell us what we needed to do next. My father showed them to me on my transistor radio and warned me not to run the batteries down.

"Always be prepared for an emergency," he told me. "Your life might depend on it."

*

Before he knew that he was dying but realized something wasn't right, my father started writing letters to the government, explaining to them how the atomic bomb was making his hair fall out and turning his teeth a rusty orange. He told them that if someone didn't do something about it, he was going to go on the radio and spill his guts. He reminded them that there were hundreds or thousands of other former soldiers who had watched bombs go off who were probably watching their own hair come out in clumps and seeing their own teeth turn a rusty orange, and all of them were probably pretty mad, too, about what was happening to them.

"And it's not just our bodies falling apart," he wrote to the generals and the senators, the president, "it's what's happened to our sense of purpose. It used to be that people would look at their lives and ask, 'Why am I here?' Now, they say, 'Why bother?'"

*

My father started spending lots of time in libraries, looking up articles about atomic testing and writing down names from the articles, names of the writers, names of the soldiers or the scientists mentioned in the stories. One of the soldiers he contacted wrote back and told my father about being in Nevada one summer and watching almost thirty atomic tests. He told my father that he had helped dress pigs in different protective outfits to see which one stood up best to an atomic blast. He told my father that sometimes he and the other soldiers were ordered to lie down in trenches and cover up before a blast, but other times they were supposed to stand at attention. When they did that, they wore goggles with black lenses and rubbed their faces with zinc oxide. He said they looked like skulls, skulls wearing helmets.

The soldier told my father that he would join him on the radio and tell about what had happened to him. He said he was angry because he was sick now due to all the radiation. But before he and my father could find someone to let them come on to their radio show, the soldier died. His wife wrote to my father and told him what had happened. "I hope you can tell people about my husband," she wrote. "He was a nice man and always tried to do the right thing. He thought the atomic bomb was the right thing. He thought it would keep everyone safe."

*

If my father had stayed alive, I think Boyd would have asked him to come onto his program to talk about his experiences. I think the two of them would have had a very good conversation about the bomb and how it could kill people years after it went off. I think a lot of people would have called in. It would have been a good program, a memorable one.

It is dawn. The round-faced boy is asleep in his bed. The radio next to him crackles with static because the man who reads the Bible every night has turned off the generator. It is time for the man to go home. His eyes burn and he rubs them with the heels of his hands. His shirt is soaked with sweat. Outside the tin building, a thin bluish ribbon of oily smoke rises from the generator. It rises into the pink morning where, in the west, the last stars burn dimly and the moon grows fainter and fainter until it is no more than a ghostly smudge. The Bible man steps out into the early light and sees the moon. To him, it looks like God's thumbprint. He thanks God for this fine day, then he gets into his car and drives home. On the way, he sees the atomic soldier pulling his wagon. He sees him every day and, every day, he asks God to have pity on the poor man.

The atomic soldier does not know he is being prayed for. He is hungry. He did not sleep well. All night, he dreamed of a boy with a round face standing over him. Behind the boy, shooting stars streaked across the sky.

Where The Roads Go

I have a map. It is a map I found in the glove compartment of my car under the owner's manual and a pile of dusty paper napkins from a drive-in restaurant. It is a map of Ohio. When I fold it out on the seat, I see that someone has traced a path in red ink along the roads. The path ends at the city of Sandusky. Sandusky is circled with the same ink many, many times, and I wonder if the person who circled it was thrilled or angry or resigned about going there. I wonder what would make a person go there in the first place.

*

I think about Sandusky. I think about the people who live there and wonder what they do. I'm sure it's a place like most places, but there has to be something that makes it different. Maybe there is a festival celebrating agriculture or the founding of the city. Maybe a religious group settled there and built a church out of limestone that can be seen for miles. Their high school football team may have once gone undefeated for eight straight seasons and on Friday nights, at home games, some of the men who played for those teams—gray-haired now but still robust—stand on the sidelines with the boys of this year's team and cheer them on. A famous actress might be from Sandusky, someone people might remember as vivacious. There could be a dog track or a botanic garden donated by a wealthy resident. An awful crime might have happened or a train wreck, a tornado, a fire, or a flood.

*

Sandusky is sinking. It is sinking and sliding into Lake Erie at the rate of one inch per year. This doesn't seem like much, but if you've lived in Sandusky for a while, you notice things. You notice that the walk from your house to your mailbox at the curb is a bit steeper now. You notice that the angle of the sun is different, which makes the light different, which makes sunsets more spectacular, especially in the fall as the days grow shorter. The days seem even shorter because of the sinking and sliding.

Parts of Sandusky are built on top of a primordial swamp. The swamp was already hidden beneath top soil when people moved in and started putting up houses and businesses, so nobody knew the danger that lurked beneath their feet. But one day, after the city was about as big as it is now, with almost as many people and almost as many tall office buildings, an entire block on McIntire Avenue just disappeared. One minute it was there. The next minute, there was just an enormous hole belching fire and dust. More than 90 people perished. A week later, before the city had a chance to recover and to think about what happened and why, another hole opened, swallowing an elementary school. Luckily, this time it happened late at night, so there was no one in the building. But there were classroom pets—hamsters and turtles, mostly—that were lost.

I look at the map and decide I will take Boyd to Sandusky. It will take us out of our way, our beeline to Tucumcari, but there is a reason that the map was in my car, in my glove compartment, a reason that I found it.

As soon as we get there, I'm going to take us to a diner and order the city's favorite food: frog legs with cheesy noodles. This has been on the menus of Sandusky's restaurants for decades.

*

When we reach farm country, fields on either side of the road will be green with whatever is planted there. The land will be mostly flat with only low hills. This is due to the glaciers smoothing the land millions of years ago, great mountains of ice grinding rocks into dirt that is good for growing things. The horizon in farm country is a straight line. It marks the exact spot where the sky and ground meet. Narrow, two-lane roads, paved with tar or covered with gravel, are straight, too. Settled in the fields, suddenly appearing after miles of tall corn crowding the road, are neatly tended farms with white houses and red barns. On Sundays, the people who live in these houses get into their cars and drive to the nearest town. If you pass one of these cars, you will see a serious-looking man in a suit and tie behind the wheel. If he is not wearing a hat, you will see that his forehead is pale while the rest of his face is weathered brown. Next to him, his wife wears a nice hat and, in the back seat, their children stare glumly out the window. This is what families around here do on Sunday mornings on their way to church. It is a joyless time, a pious time, a time to cast back over what they have done that week, good and bad, and to figure out if their lives have been changed by something that happened, something that they did. As a rule, not much of consequence has occurred.

*

So much of what Boyd and I will see will look familiar. I will see things I recognize and point them out. A mailbox made to look like an airplane at the top of a tall pole. A gravel road curving between two hills. I will even see a man on a front porch that I'm sure I've seen before. He waves, lifting a hand from the elbow in a palm-out salute. I will tell Boyd that we should stop and talk to him. I will tell Boyd that I did stop one time and talk to him. His name is Leland and he told me that he had recently retired from a long career as a rural mail carrier. I asked him about the airplane mailbox and he says that's nothing. The Finches, who live just up that road there, have a mailbox shaped like an igloo, why in God's name, I don't know.

*

Some evening, when the sun has already dropped below the horizon, we will drive into a town that is having a celebration. There's a ferris wheel in the middle of the main street, along with a few other rides, games of chance and food stands. Strings of light bulbs are stretched overhead. Because of the celebration, we are sent on a detour that takes us past the backs of the businesses and past houses. The houses are old and grand. A couple of them are three stories tall, and one of them has white columns like a southern plantation. The people on the street will smile and wave as they make their way to the celebration, and I think how nice it would be to stop and join in. But we won't be able to do that. We'll be on our way to Tucumcari and in a hurry.

*

Another day, we will be driving through a forest. The road winds through trees that grow right next to the asphalt. There is no shoulder to speak of. It will have rained recently, and the trees will be black and wet. Moss stands out against the black trunks in patches of green and white. On one side of the road, the trees pull back, and we will see a cabin. A woman is standing outside. She is wearing a blue dress. In one hand, she holds a knife. In the other, she holds a headless chicken. We see a child coming from behind the cabin. The woman turns toward the child. Then the trees close in again.

*

Once I pulled into a gas station and met a man named Nestor Crabbe. He told me he was related to the famous Buster Crabbe who starred in Tarzan movies. It was his gas station, Nestor's. He had owned it for 37 years but was going to retire from the business at the end of the next month. No one wanted to buy the place—few travelers got this far off the main road—so he was going to set it on fire. "All my life," he told me, "I been afraid something'd spark and blow me to kingdom come. That's why I got to burn this place down. I gotta get rid of being afraid all the time."

*

You meet many interesting people on the road. I wonder sometimes if they are as interesting when they're at home. I wonder sometimes if personalities change when people get away from home. That would explain why people buy souvenirs and wear odd hats or find themselves thinking thoughts they never knew they had.

For example, the Tartabulls from Hendersonville, Kentucky, Karl and Emma. They were driving a bus that they had converted into a house on wheels and were towing a little car behind. They were both very small and wore large black plastic sunglasses that fit right over their regular glasses. They didn't know exactly where they were going, but that didn't matter because they were retired and didn't have any children. Each day they would get up and one of them would ask the other, "Where to?" And the other one had to say the first thing that came to mind. "I wouldn't mind exploring a cave today" or "What say we visit a dairy farm?" or "I'm in the mood for some local history." Some days, they just stayed wherever it was that they were staying and sat outside on lawn chairs and talked to people who were staying there, too.

*

Also, I met a woman who said she was a psychic. Whenever something happens, she said she knew it was going to happen. I asked her if she could predict something before it happens, but she said no because that would be an improper way to use her gift. She said her gift of being able to see that something was meant to happen after it had happened was more special than being able to predict the future because she can see the big picture, not just one event.

"Like meeting you," she said. "It's part of a larger thing, a larger pattern."

"What's the pattern?" I asked.

"Wait and see," she said. "You have to wait and see."

Her name was Cindy and she had to use drops in her eyes because her tear ducts didn't work. She worked in a drive-in restaurant that didn't have carhops anymore, even though you still pulled your car in nose first under a wide awning.

A lot of people miss carhops but I always felt uncomfortable ordering because the carhop would lean in so that she could hear you, and if you turned your head to help her hear you, your mouths were just inches apart.

It was easy to fall in love in those situations.

*

Once Boyd and I are on the road, out on a highway with wide lanes and a clear view, I'll lean back against the seat and feel the road hum beneath me. I will pass cars. Cars will pass me. I will sing along with the radio even though I don't know any of the songs.

The miles will just disappear behind us.

The National System of Interstate and Defense Highways was inspired by the autobahn in Germany during World War II and was started because President Eisenhower wanted a way to move military equipment and soldiers around as quickly as the Germans did. He was concerned that if the Russians attacked, convoys would be caught in traffic jams or waiting for lights to change, so he had his engineers come up with a design that would eliminate any delays that might cause us to lose a war. What they came up with was a plan to build 41,000 miles of four-lane divided highways that would cross the country east and west and north and south.

The roads would also provide quick evacuation routes in case of an atomic attack.

Each of the lanes of these highways would be 12 feet wide.

Each right shoulder would be 10 feet wide and each left shoulder would be three feet wide.

The median was to be no less than 36 feet wide. Access to the highways would be limited to ramp entrances and exits, and there would be no gas stations or other businesses allowed to be built right next to the roadway.

The National System of Interstate and Defense Highways also required that one mile in every five must be straight. These straight sections would be used as airstrips in times of war or other emergencies.

*

The man who was responsible for picking the colors of the interstate highway signs that would tell people where they were and how far it was to the next exit ramp was named Bertram Tallamy. He wanted the road signs to be blue with white letters. He thought that was the best combination even though he was color blind. People who could see color picked green and white instead.

*

In California, a group of engineers suggested atomic bombs be used to vaporize part of the Bristol Mountains because they were slowing completion of Interstate 40 through that part of the state. The plan was to detonate bombs that would be 133 times as powerful as the bombs dropped on Hiroshima and Nagasaki and would produce a mushroom cloud 12,000 feet high.

There would be special seating for VIPs who wanted to watch.

*

Those engineers thought it would be all right to disintegrate mountains because President Eisenhower and his

106

advisors were looking for ways to use atomic bombs other than killing people. He was looking for ways to use atomic bombs because the United States had so many of them that the world was worried that the whole planet could be destroyed. President Eisenhower called this plan "Atoms for Peace."

Part of "Atoms for Peace" was Operation Plowshare. Operation Plowshare was created to come up with practical uses for atomic bombs. Scientists and engineers came up with a list of projects they thought would work:

Change weather patterns by exploding a bomb in the eye of a hurricane.

Build harbors.

Excavate for oil and natural gas.

Melt the polar ice caps

Build a bigger and better Panama Canal.

*

When a bomb was detonated nearly a mile underground in New Mexico to reach deep natural gas pockets, it left a crater 80 feet across and 335 feet deep. Wells were drilled, but the gas was too radioactive to use, so they filled in the crater and warned people not to go there anymore.

*

Another part of "Atoms for Peace" was an exhibition showing how atomic bombs could be put to good use. The exhibition was sent all over the world to reassure people that the United States was sincere in how it was going to use its atomic bombs.

One of the places the exhibition traveled to was Hiroshima.

Sidetrack

Sometimes I worry that I won't make it to Tucumcari. Not that I won't make it, but that I'll decide not to go after all. That is why I'm driving to Tucumcari, but, in the end, I won't end up in Tucumcari. At some point, at a rest stop or a restaurant, a gas station, a motel, I'll drive away and leave Boyd. I'll veer north and wind up in a town on the Canadian border, a place where the snow is real, very deep, and falls every day from October to May. In this land of white softness, I will buy a cabin, chop my own wood, go to town once a week for groceries and to stop off at the library. I will have a dog, Rusty.

On the coldest nights of the year, I will drag my mattress in front of the fireplace and sleep there. The cabin will have no electricity except for what I produce with my portable generator, which I will use very sparingly and usually when I want to heat up water for a bath. I will have a battery powered radio, a very powerful one, so I can listen to stations in Quebec and Arkansas. I will learn how to hunt, how to track deer, how to walk in snowshoes, how to field dress. I will plunge my hands into the slit belly of a doe to warm my fingers. I will grow a beard, go to town dances, meet a woman who lives like me. Her name will be Audrey, and we will be married, but we will continue to live in our separate cabins seven miles apart across two rivers. We will talk on the phone once a week and share a bed two or three days a month, depending upon the weather, one of us tramping across the snow or, in those rare green months, across a rocky portage trail. I will die happy and innocent, frozen beneath a limb that fell on me. My last thoughts will be of Audrey and Boyd.

It's Not What You Know

One of the jobs my father had was selling encyclopedias but not the famous encyclopedias like *The World Book* or *Encyclopedia Britannica*. The encyclopedia my father sold was *Cochrane's Encyclopedia of Complete Knowledge*, which was written entirely by people named Cochrane. Sets of *Cochrane's Encyclopedia of Complete Knowledge* came in different colors and different bindings. My father had sales copies of each one, thin versions of the real books filled with examples of the kinds of entries you would get when you bought all 24 volumes. The most expensive set was dark blue leather with gold lettering. The pages were edged in gold as well. The next most expensive was red. It had gold lettering, too, but the cover only looked like leather, and the pages weren't gold. The cheapest set was covered in scratchy brown cloth and had black lettering. The pages were thick and stiff and didn't seem to hold the ink as well as the other two. And there were no color illustrations. No color plates, no overlays of the human body you could turn back one by one to reveal the secrets inside. The least expensive had only black and white drawings and prints and photographs, which made gaining complete knowledge a dreary thought.

To show him how to sell *Cochrane's Encyclopedia of Complete Knowledge,* the company, which was based in Baltimore, Maryland, provided my father with the sample copies. They also sent him some leaflets that emphasized how important these volumes would be to schoolchildren and a phonograph record of instruction. The first side of the record had successful salesmen talking about how they went about going door to door and winning over people who never seemed to want a set of encyclopedias. These successful salesmen seemed to have almost magical powers of persuasion that transformed even the most reluctant potential customers into eager buyers, none of whom bought the brown set. Everyone on the record sold the blue and maybe a red now and then, here and there. On the other side of the record, actors pretending to be salesmen and people who answered the doorbell played out simulations of sales calls. There were all kinds of examples: the nervous salesman and the over-confident salesman, the under-prepared, the easily-defeated, the Lothario, the old pro, the sad sack. At the end of each scene, a man with a very deep voice would tell the actor playing the salesman what he needed to do to be better at selling encyclopedias. Even the old pro could improve sales with a little extra effort, the extra mile.

My father didn't last long selling *Cochrane's Encyclopedia of*

Complete Knowledge because most people wanted the well-known encyclopedias that everyone else was buying. When he finally gave up and shipped everything back to Maryland, he kept the cloth-covered sample copy and gave it to me. Because the articles in the sample copy were only examples and not complete, I only learned some of what I might have learned but I spent many hours reading and could answer questions in school that my classmates could not, even though their families probably had full sets of encyclopedias .

*

If I had gotten a full set, I think I could have been a Junior Genius on the radio.

Junior Geniuses were children from all over the country who competed against each other for money to go to college. The oldest one on the program when I listened was 12 and the youngest one was Emerson Bean, the Egghead Baby. Emerson Bean was eight years old, but he had been amazing since birth. At the age of one, he learned to speak Spanish and how to read. When he was three, he could do algebra. Because he was so smart, he skipped all of elementary school and junior high and enrolled, at age six, in a private high school. Even though he was so smart, he would miss a question on Junior Geniuses, which would surprise everyone, including the Quiz Master, Professor H. T. Pythagoras. Some long-time listeners called in to say that Emerson was giving the wrong answer on purpose. They wondered if he was just feeling sorry for the other children or if the show was rigged. I never found out what happened because we moved again, and I couldn't pick up the program on any of the stations that came in on my transistor.

When I did listen, though, I could answer some questions even before Emerson Bean pushed his buzzer button. The ones I could answer were things I had read about in the book my father had given me. Sometimes, though, I couldn't answer a question on a subject I had read about because the information they were looking for must have been in the part of the encyclopedia entry that came after the example in my book ended.

*

A few years ago, I found an article in a magazine about Emerson Bean, the Egghead Baby. The article had an old photograph of him in college. He was only 10, but he was surrounded by cheerleaders who were hugging him and kissing the top of his over-sized head. Emerson Bean was smiling, but you could tell he wasn't enjoying himself all that much. He was reaching out for someone who wasn't in the picture, someone who could rescue him from all of the hugging and kissing, all of the attention.

*

When he was older and had been working on secret projects for the government for a while, Boyd had him on his radio program. They didn't talk about the secret projects, which would have been interesting, too, but about being a Junior Genius on the radio. Emerson Bean said that, before the radio program, he had been driven around the country by his father to take part in intelligence contests, which were a very popular attraction at state and county fairs.

Because Emerson Bean was so much smarter than the other children in the local contests, rules were changed so that only those who lived in the county or the state were allowed to enter. Emerson Bean's father was so outraged by the discrimination that he filed a lawsuit against the State of Nebraska. The lawsuit brought lots of attention to Emerson Bean, lots of newspaper stories and lots of photographs. A radio producer who had the idea for Junior Geniuses read one of the stories and thought that Emerson would be a great addition to the program. On Boyd's show, Emerson Bean said that he had never really liked being pitted against other, less brainy children. He said it only pointed out how different he was from them and it made him feel lonely.

"I did not have one friend growing up," Emerson Bean said to Boyd. "I spent my entire childhood watching other children play and have fun. All I did was read and answer questions." When Boyd asked him if he gave a wrong answer on purpose, Emerson

Bean wouldn't tell him. "It was such a long time ago now, I just don't remember. I do remember, however, that my father was never happy when I missed an answer. There were consequences."

My Mother's Travel Plans

My mother never liked our moving around but she always wanted to travel. She wanted to go to some place she had planned to go to ahead of time. She wanted to go to some place she might have read about or that was the setting of a movie. She wanted a guidebook with all of the famous places marked and a map to get her to each one. She wanted to see things she could never imagine and learn things that she had never known. *This is the home of a wealthy merchant who murdered his wife because she was too beautiful. Over there, down that narrow, cobblestone alley, is a fountain people believed for centuries flowed with healing waters. Just past that archway is the tomb of a saint, the tomb of a national hero, the tomb of a revered painter.* She did not just want to visit places that were foreign. She wanted to go to places that were mysterious, places with a secret she thought she might be able to figure out, given time.

*

The place she wanted to visit most was Easter Island. She wanted to see for herself the big stone heads, put her hand on one, have her picture taken with it. She read a lot about the statues and told me once that the people who put them up believed that they represented dead ancestors and that if they made sacrifices to those ancestors, they would be taken care of. Something must have gone wrong, though, because after a while, they stopped believing in the statues and believed instead in the Birdman.

The Birdman was picked every year in a contest. If you had a dream that you might be the Birdman, you jumped into the ocean with all of the other men who had the same dream. Then, you swam to a little island where you had to find a seagull egg and then swim back to the big island without losing it or breaking it or getting eaten by sharks. All of those things happened quite a bit, apparently. The first one back to the big island had to climb up a cliff and hand it to another man who had shaved his head and painted his skull either red or white. Then the new Birdman led a parade down the other side of the cliff to a special house where he spent the year alone, letting his fingernails grow and wearing a headdress made of human hair.

The problem with both religions was that the people thought someone else was going to take care of them, either a dead relative or a hermit with long fingernails, so they forgot how to take care of themselves, how to plan ahead. They chopped down all of the trees to make houses. They ate up all of the fruits and vegetables without ever bothering to plant any more. They ate up all of the animals and birds. Finally, they started eating each other.

"Let that be a lesson," my mother said.

*

My mother read about Easter Island when we would go to a library so that my father could find out things about the atomic bomb to put in his letters to the government. Sometimes she would read guide books and sometimes she would read stories written by people who traveled, stories about what they saw and did, diaries of their adventures. She said that she liked the books with facts and pictures better than the diaries but she read the diaries sometimes just to see what people's reactions were to a place she didn't think she would ever want to visit. That way, she said, she could get a feel for being in a strange land or a strange city without giving away what she would find when she got to a place she wanted to visit.

When she is not working as a house cleaner, the young woman takes care of her parents. Her father's heart is going bad and her mother has lost the ability to think clearly. They still sleep in the same bed but when they were awake, each of them has a different room where they spend the day. Her father reads newspapers and listens to radio talk shows and her mother takes a great deal of time rearranging family photo albums. The young woman drifts from room to room and makes sure they are comfortable. She fixes lunch for them and checks to see that they are covered when they fall asleep in their chairs in the afternoons. While they sleep, she sits in the living room and reads, expecting at any moment to hear her name called. She reads whole books without recollecting a word because she is always listening. When they die, first her father and then her mother, within two weeks of each other, she cleans their rooms and then looks again at her stack of books, all read, none remembered, and starts in anew.

Let That Be A Lesson

The class I teach for people who want to learn English meets at night, which means I have to put rolls of coins in my pockets to keep myself grounded. Quarters, usually. We meet in a classroom in a junior high building, a building made of the same red brick that the factories are made of. The number and faces change so often, sometimes I think I have wandered into the wrong room or I came on the wrong day. One night, there may be six students, all broad-faced members of the same family and, another night, there will be more students than chairs.

*

The room where I teach belongs to Norma Norman. Norma Norman is a 7th grade social studies teacher and her classroom walls are covered with maps and charts and pictures of people from all over the world. Because of the things on the walls, this is a good room for my class. My students can go to a map and put a finger on the place they are from. They can see a face that looks

121

like their face, a smile they remember. For that reason, I am happy to be in Norma Norman's room.

But I think Norma Norman hates me. I think she is bothered by the fact that my class meets in her room. I think she is afraid we will break something or create disorder of some kind, chaos. Every week when I get to the room, there is a note written on the blackboard: *Do Not Erase!* Some weeks, there are notes or questions covering the board (*Where did Magellan die? How long is the Great Wall of China?*), other nights she has just written page numbers for her students, pages for them to read. There is still a little space on those occasions but she has also locked the chalk in her desk, so I don't have anything to write with anyway. Because I can't use the chalkboard, I have to find another way to let my students know what the words they are trying to learn look like. I found a large tablet of paper in a closet and was able to use that before the closet was locked, too.

Now I bring objects small enough to fit in a grocery sack and set them out on the desk. I pick up each one, tell the students what it is, and then they say the word. Almost everything I bring is something from my own apartment.

*

Some nights, I bring *Cochrane's Encyclopedia of Complete Knowledge*, just in case someone asks a question or a situation arises which allows me to look up the answer. Once, a woman who attended class with her husband came in wearing a silver, perforated cup taped over one eye. When I asked her what happened, she undid the tape and showed me how purple and swollen her eye had become, how it was oozing something yellow.

This gave me a chance to consult my *Cochrane's*, which has an entry on the human eye. I could not find anything about her condition but I did talk about eye safety. I told them to never look directly into a very bright light, especially the sun, because it can burn out your rods and cones. If you burn out your rods and cones, I warned them, you will only be able to see the world in black and white. The only time you'll ever see color again is when you dream.

*

Tonight, there are nine students in the room when I arrive. I only recognize two, though it's possible that they have all been here before. I have an attendance sheet printed with names I can't pronounce. Every six weeks, I turn in the sheet and am given another one. Like the one before it, I will fill the new one out just before I turn it in because I can't see any point in marking down who came and who didn't.

We have just started to review last week's words (*soup, ladle, bowl, spoon*) when two young men in identical pale blue tunics come in. They bow and smile and say, in unison, "So sorry for the interruption. I was delayed by circumstances beyond my control." Their pronunciation is not as clear as I'd like it to be but I am pleased that they understand that this is the right situation for an apology. I have taught my students many apologies because it's important to be sorry for something that you've done or that you didn't do.

*

When I first started teaching, I would tell my students stories. It was another way for them to learn. Some nights, I spent the whole time telling stories. My students sat and listened. They were very attentive and occasionally asked questions.

"Where is the man from?"

"Who is his name?"

"Is Audrey knowing he is coming? Does she know?"

Lately, I have taken to reading my mother's stories to my students at the end of the evening. I will read a sentence or two and then stop to wait for the ones who understood what I read to explain to those who don't. Most of the time, when I reach the end, they clap their hands. They want to meet my mother and thank her for the wonderful stories and are very sad when I tell them that she had died.

This is their favorite story. If I read them something

different, they ask for this one, too, even though it means that class will run late:

A cool breeze came down from the north just before dawn. It moved curtains as it blew into bedrooms and kitchens. A woman pulled a blanket up and covered herself. A man getting ready for work cocked his head and held his hand up, feeling the air. Dogs scratched at doors, asking to be let in.

The breeze kept up all morning and gray clouds slid south, smelling of rain. People watched the storm come. They stopped work and went out into the street to wait. Lightning rippled deep in the clouds. Thunder rumbled, rattling windows.

When the rain started, it fell like stones, heavy as hail, denting cars and leaving welts on the faces of those who tipped their heads up and opened their mouths. Electricity shot across the wires that drooped from poles in alleys and along residential streets. Television picture tubes and light bulbs exploded, refrigerators turned everything inside into chunks of ice, telephones melted, the conveyor belts in the chicken plant threw plucked carcasses at the wall, and the

Presbyterian Church caught fire.

When the rain ended and the sky cleared, flowers bloomed everywhere. The desert was a blanket of red and yellow and patches of blue. A train passed through the flowers, snatching petals as it went, petals that swirled in the wake of the locomotive and filled the air with sweet perfume.

*

After class, when I ride the bus and all of the stores' signs are lit up, I can see where an area with people from one country switches to an area with people who have come here from a different country. For one thing, the alphabet changes. Some of the letters don't seem like letters at all. Even though I can't read the signs, I can tell what kind of business is being advertised because there is also a picture of some kind—a coat hanger, a chicken—but other times I don't even have a guess. The people at night dress in clothes from their part of the world rather than the uniforms they wear during the day.

*

When I get home after my class, I am too keyed up to go sleep, so I go up onto the roof of my building and lie there, looking at the stars. I am above the light from the streets, the streetlights, above the neon signs, so I can see the familiar shapes of constellations, the faint spread of the Milky Way behind them.

I never learned the constellations. I couldn't see all of the patterns, and I couldn't remember the names, so I made up my own. I connected stars and gave them names: The Big House, The Little House, Somebody's Cat, Pretty Dancer, Cowboy Hat, The Umbrella.

When Boyd was still on the radio, he admitted that he didn't know the constellations, either.

It's another thing we have in common, another thing we can talk about.

The Man I Can See From My Window

This morning, the sun seems faint. The light seems faint. Not diffused. There are no clouds, so it's not diffused. It's faint, like a 40-watt light bulb in a reading lamp. Inadequate. Faint. Weak. Like the day ahead will be just too much to bear, so it's saving its energy, saving up so it's got enough if there's really a need for it. As for me, the faint light has an effect. It's made me buoyant. When I take a step, I push off and make an arc in the air. I feel like I look like ballet dancers look when they leap, but I'm not leaping. I just take a step and describe a slow, low, graceful arc. And when I land, it's like landing on a pillow or particularly loamy soil. There's a give, a softness.

*

The man across the street who stays inside all day and works jigsaw puzzles is waiting for a phone call. I can see a telephone next to his chair. I can see him glancing over at it, sometimes putting a hand on the receiver. Maybe he's not waiting for a phone call, maybe he is trying to work up enough courage to make a phone call. Maybe that's why he lays a hand on the receiver, lifts it, settles it back in its cradle.

*

The man across the street has information he needs to pass along. He knows something that others need to know but he can't bring himself to telephone the authorities. Part of him wants to get rid of the burden of knowing what he knows, of getting it into the right hands so he can begin to live again, but another part of him is frightened that he'll be found out. He's not sure what to do next, except to put in another piece of the jigsaw puzzle, this time the crest of a wave in a seascape where a three-masted ship is being tossed and battered.

*

The man across the street has broken up with his wife after 17 years of marriage. He expects her to call any day now to patch things up, to start over.

*

The man across the street who works jigsaw puzzles is afraid to leave his apartment. He is sure if he leaves his apartment, something terrible will happen to him, something he can do nothing to prevent. This fear can cause him to have a panic attack, which is

129

another thing he is afraid of.

The telephone is his only link to the world but he is also afraid to answer it, which is why, every time it rings, he lifts the receiver and then puts it back down.

He thinks about getting rid of his telephone but, if he does, how will anyone get a hold of him?

*

Above the man who never leaves his apartment, on the roof of his building, is a billboard for a new brand of perfume. It's called Amok. The woman holding the bottle of perfume is Belladonna Clinch, the most beautiful woman in the world.

Why is there a billboard for perfume in a neighborhood of men? To entice them to buy it for women they don't know? Women in their future? Women who would appreciate a bottle of perfume rather than a steak dinner and a few drinks? Those women do not live around here, and the only way that the men who live near me could ever meet a woman of that kind would be to hop a bus and go to that part of the city where there are nightclubs and movie theaters and bowling alleys. They would have to hop a different bus just to buy the perfume. You would never find it in this neighborhood.

One Less Thing

This is the day.

This is the day I leave for Tucumcari. The day Boyd and I go.

I am ready.

Nearly ready. But there are things I still need to do. I have a list. Each time I cross something off, it is one less thing I have to do before I can leave. But I am adding things too, so the list is nearly as long as it was when I first made it. Most of them won't take much time—close and lock the windows, put furniture back the way I found it—but others will require more from me. They will require that I take a bus and walk and climb stairs or ride elevators and that I will have to deal with people who have jobs that have hardened them and made them impatient and cross. These people need to be visited before I leave. Earlier encounters lead me to believe that just showing up at their offices will irk them.

The worst people are postal employees. They are the ones

who seem most vexed whenever someone answers their call—"Next!"—and steps forward with a package or an envelope. Each person is made to feel that he or she is intruding on the postal worker's otherwise pleasant life. I need to go to the post office to fill out a change of address card even though I don't know what my new address will be and I never receive any mail. I do it because of the atomic bomb and the need for someone to know where I'm supposed to be, in case I'm one of those vaporized in the blast. Or not. Then a change of address card will be even more important because then Audrey could find me and wouldn't worry.

*

Once a month, at the end of every month, I go to the business district to pay the rent on my apartment. I join the men at the bus station who make the trip every day and I try to blend in. I have a rolled up newspaper tucked under my arm and I look down, scowling. Occasionally, I will look at my watch and say, under my breath but loud enough, "Late."

When the bus arrives, I find an open seat near the middle, slide in next to the window and keep my face turned to the glass the whole way. If someone sits next to me, I can feel his weight as he drops onto the seat, hear his sigh, but I don't know what he looks like. It could be the same person every month for all I know.

The bus lurches and shakes and hisses along its route, stopping only four times before I get off. I am lucky because the bus stops right in front of my bank, so I hop off, go in and withdraw the money I need and deliver it to my landlord's office. If there aren't many people in line at the bank or on the sidewalk, I can complete my errand, have a cup of coffee and a cheese Danish at Fred's Deluxe Diner, and be back home in less than an hour.

Because I am going to Tucumcari, I make an extra trip to the business district today, to my landlord's office to tell them that I am leaving and to get my damage deposit money back. Usually, when I get to the office, I deal with a pleasant young woman named Trish who takes my money, counts it, makes out a receipt and sends me on my way with a smile and a cheerful "See you next month!" On this day, though, which is not my usual day of the week to visit the office, Trish is not working. Instead, at her desk behind the counter, there is a young man with black curly hair and black-framed glasses. He looks up at me. I wait for him to speak but he just looks at me, blinking. I notice that his ink pen has leaked in the pocket of his yellow shirt. I wonder if I should point it out. I wonder if he already knows.

"What do you need?" he says finally. "Are you paying rent?"

"No, actually, I'm here to get my damage deposit. I'm leaving my apartment. I'm going away. Leaving the city."

"I can't give you the deposit until the property has been inspected for damage."

"There's no damage. I haven't done anything to the place. No damage at all."

"Someone has to inspect the place." He looks at a calendar. "Mr. Murdoch can fit you in next Wednesday." He stands, picks up a clipboard and hands it to me. "Write the address of the building and your apartment number here. Would you prefer a morning or an afternoon inspection?"

I tell him that afternoon is fine, even though I will be long gone. When I finish with the clipboard, he takes it back, looks at what I've written and then drops it back on his desk.

"You need to know that these inspections are very thorough and that you will be charged for any damage that Mr. Murdoch finds."

"There isn't any—"

"Even a scratch. Even a tiny, tiny scratch." He shows me with his thumb and forefinger just how tiny.

I start to say something about scratches but I am interrupted.

"And when you leave," the young man says, "you need to return both keys here, to this office."

"I didn't get two keys. I have one key. Just the one."

"Every apartment has two keys. You are responsible for two. If you only have one, you'll have to pay for the other."

*

I read somewhere that 90% of all landlords are social misfits. They don't know how to make friends and they don't come from good families, so they consider their renters their family members or their friends, and then they mistreat them as a way to get back at all of the people who were miserable to them during their lives.

It might not have been 90%. It might have been lower.

*

Because I am leaving, I decide I need to get a haircut. I know the shop may be busy and I may have to wait before I can get my hair cut, but when I get to Tucumcari and see Audrey again, I want to look well-groomed.

I go into the barbershop and a man reading a magazine looks up at me. He slides over to make room. I am surprised that besides the two of us waiting our turn, the only other people in the place are the barber and a man in the barber's chair.

The man in the chair has a striped cloth around his neck and only a few patches of yellowish hair on his head. There is so little hair on the man's head that the barber cannot even hold it with his comb, so he just runs the comb through the man's hair and then snips the air above the man's head. The man is watching all of this in a mirror that runs the length of one wall. He doesn't seem to mind what the barber is doing. A radio on the marble counter behind the barber is playing a song I've heard before. The singer is a woman and she's singing about a man. The man in the song has left her and now she wants him to come back. It's a sad song but the tune is upbeat.

"I know you." The man with the magazine is looking at me. He points at me with his thumb. "You're Phillips."

A fluorescent tube overhead hums loudly. Then there is a kind of crackling noise and the light goes out. The man sitting next to me looks up. The barber and the man in the chair look up. I look up. The burned-out tube is gray and dead.

"No," I say to the man with the magazine. "I'm Watts."

I'm not Watts but I would never give my real name to a stranger in a barbershop.

"I could swear you were Phillips."

"No, sorry. I'm Watts."

"There was another guy in here before. He wasn't Phillips, either."

"Who was he?"

"Name was something like Frazier or Farmer. Something like that."

"Fairchild?"

"Might've been Fairchild."

"What did he look like?"

"I don't know. I'm better with names than faces."

I turn and look out the window.

*

Sometimes when we were together, maybe raking leaves or walking to the grocery store, my father would push my shoulder and say, "Run!"

"Why?"

"It doesn't matter why. Just run." And then he would drop his rake or let go of my hand and sprint away, never looking back to see if I was coming too.

This was his drill, his teaching me to be nimble and alert and to take off as fast as I could whenever something felt wrong. Not quite right.

What My Parents Left Behind

Because we didn't stay in one place very long, we didn't accumulate much in the way of earthly possessions. All of what I have from my parents is in one cardboard box.

Here's the inventory:

1. Two containers of ashes (wooden, rectangular)
2. My father's military souvenirs (medals and commendations, sleeve patches, diary)
3. My mother's stories and letters
4. Travel books
5. Gold-plated cigarette lighter
6. My mother's jewelry box with a few rings and necklaces and pins
7. Packet of recipes on index cards bound with a rubber band
8. Photo album, mostly empty
9. Piece of trinitite
10. Penny flattened by a train (year indecipherable)

11. Men's hairbrush

12. Rabbit's foot on a beaded chain

13. Fountain pen (tortoise shell, expensive)

14. Pocket knife (one blade broken)

*

I also have my mother's typewriter, which doesn't fit in the box. I forgot to mention that. It comes in its own carrying case.

*

I traveled alone a lot after my mother died. Some of it was for work but some of it wasn't. Sometimes it just seemed right to be driving with my parents' ashes in the back seat, seeing new places. Most of the time, I didn't have a destination in mind. I would drive and think and end up somewhere. If I was lucky, it would be a place I had never been before.

*

"What have we here?" my father would say when he was alive and driving us to places we had never been before.

"Watson: Home of the Gourd Festival."

"Catlow: The Biggest Little Town Around."

"I think this is an alpaca ranch. See, out there? Those are alpacas."

"They're getting ready for a rodeo, I'm guessing."

"Let's stop. I could use a root beer float."

*

When I used to travel alone, I would listen to Boyd on the radio. Before he got sick, no matter where I was, I could find a station that carried his program. It was one night in the car that I heard Boyd talking with an expert on improbability. It was his opinion that the universe is more random than we like to believe, so we invent reasons for things happening the way they do rather than chalking it up to luck. "Stories are the best tool we have for making sense of all the things that don't fit into our understanding of the world," he said. "Stories are built on cause and effect and a clear sense of chronology and reason. Stories keep us from feeling helpless and not in control, even though we are both of those things."

This may not be exactly what the expert said. When I was listening, there was static, quite a bit of static. Finally, I got too far away and lost the signal altogether.

*

I remember the evenings Osseo Fairchild called in, but I don't remember what his voice sounded like or what he said exactly. If I had, I would have tried to memorize his voice and see if I could recall patterns in his choice of words or the way he

140

organized sentences. If I could do that, I'd be able to pick him out and keep him from going after Boyd.

It's possible, too, to figure out a person's size by the sound of their voice, by the way it reverberates. Small people, for example, tend to have tinny voices because their rib cages are not cushioned with muscle or fatty tissue, while large, heavy-set people have thicker voices, more mellifluous. When Boyd was at his peak in popularity, he was also at his peak, size-wise, and he sounded better. Toward the end of his time on the radio, if you didn't know it was Boyd, you'd never have guessed it was him. His voice was raspy and weak, and there were times when the words didn't even make it to the microphone. They floated up and away like wisps of smoke.

*

My parents wanted to be cremated. They wanted to be cremated mainly because they didn't know where they would want to be buried. We didn't stay in one place long enough for it to feel like home, so they wrote into their wills that they wanted to be cremated and that I was supposed to decide what to do with their ashes.

When people are cremated, their bodies are wrapped in plastic and tied with heavy twine and then put into a cardboard carton that is sealed with packing tape. After that, the carton is put into an oven heated to 2000 degrees. Partway through the process, the oven door is opened so that a worker can break up the bones into smaller pieces. When the oven is turned off and the temperature goes down enough, a worker scoops the bones into a metal container where they are left to cool completely. After that, they are put into a stainless steel grinder and pulverized. From there, they go to the funeral home where they are put into an urn and given to whomever is responsible for them.

I am surprised by how heavy my parents' ashes are. Even out of the wooden boxes, in just the thick plastic bags, they weigh a lot more than I thought they would. I don't take them out very often. The only times are when I come to someplace I know that they liked, someplace where we were happy, and I leave some ashes behind. I have to be careful about leaving ashes, especially if it's near a house where we lived, because people don't like the idea.

In The Direction of Motion

Years from now, I will look back on this day and tell
Audrey again how I knew that it was time to get Boyd and set
out for Tucumcari. Audrey will be in the next room and our son,
Rusty, will be playing in the yard with our dog. I will be watching
Rusty through the front door screen. He is laughing, and the dog
is barking. In the distance, across the desert, above the mountains,
clouds pile up thick and black. Lightning fires inside the clouds,
making them glow briefly.

"I knew he was close," I say to Audrey, meaning Osseo
Fairchild. "Practically around the corner. If I didn't get out of
there then, I don't know if I'd made it out at all."

"Well, I'm glad you did, darlin'," Audrey says over the
clatter of her potter's wheel, the chatter of her sewing machine, the
whir of her egg beater. "I don't know if I could've waited much
longer."

*

My car is covered with ash, of course, an inch or so, but it's easy to brush off with a broom. I especially need to brush off the windshield with a broom because if I use the wipers and spray the glass with wiper fluid, the ash turns to gray mud and smears. Then I have to get out of the car and wipe away the wet mess with an old towel.

There are men in the neighborhood who make a living cleaning windshields for people who try to use their wipers and wiper fluid. The men live in a hotel right next to the factory district, and they drift up and down the streets like ghosts, their hair gray and matted, their faces caked with ash, their long coats and worn shoes caked with ash. They carry bottles with a special cleaner that cuts through the smeary mess on a windshield. They are the only ones with the special cleaner and they share the secret with no one except each other.

I am so careful in brushing the ash off my car that the man with the bottle of cleaner walking toward me doesn't even bother to ask if I need help. He passes right on by, his feet scuffing crooked trails in the ash on the sidewalk.

My car starts right up when I turn the key. It starts right up and then belches a cloud of blue smoke from the exhaust pipe before settling into a steady, comforting rumble. I push on the gas pedal a couple of times to get the engine warm and to hear it roar. I put on my turn signal. I look in the side mirror to see if the street's clear. There are no cars coming, so I put my car into drive, crank the steering wheel and pull away from the curb.

*

The neighborhood where I used to live, where Boyd lives again now, is on the other side of the city, through the business district and beyond neighborhoods where the wealthy live in gigantic houses made out of stone and brick that sit back from the street, hidden behind walls of stone and brick. One Halloween, Boyd and I walked to this neighborhood because we thought we could be able to fill our sacks with exotic treats that only rich people knew about and could afford. But when we got there and started going from one place to the next, we discovered they all had black iron gates, locked iron gates, and we couldn't get in anywhere. I remember Boyd holding on to one of the gates with both hands and looking in at the gigantic house and saying to me, "We came a long way for nothing, didn't we?" I shook my paper grocery bag and had to agree.

"Still," Boyd said, "I liked getting here."

*

A long trip like this one is more than a trip. It's more like a quest. It is a quest. It fits the definition of a quest. Which means that what happens will be significant and symbolic. It means that our adventures on the road will be connected and that they will add up to something.

I'll need to be alert. If I miss something, no matter how small, it will throw the whole thing off. It will send it in another direction altogether.

I should already be alert. I might have already started the quest. It might have started when I put my car in gear and pulled away from the curb.

What did I see? A man on the corner. When he looked at me, did he hold up his hand with a finger pointed at the sky? If he did, what was he pointing at?

A sign in front of a church advertising an upcoming sermon seems too obvious to mean anything, but those blackbirds flying above the church might be writing a message. An open manhole could be an omen. So could the piece of newspaper in the gutter or the phone booth with no phone, only a tangle of wires.

There's so much to keep track of.

*

When I finally get to my old neighborhood and turn down my old street, nothing is the way I remember it. In my memory, there are more trees, and the houses are more brightly painted. The sidewalks are smooth and flat, perfect for bicycles and pulling a wagon full of returnable pop bottles. It doesn't really surprise me that I haven't recollected things accurately, but I am disappointed. I was hoping it would be the way I wanted it to be.

*

I get to my old neighborhood and my old street. I turn at the corner where a grocery store used to be. We would go there and get penny candy and wax lips and beef jerky. It was where we would take the returnable pop bottles. But it's gone now. Now there's a new building on the spot, low and built of sand-colored brick, and it's occupied by an insurance agency and a dentist.

I drive past what has to be my old house. I drive slowly so I can look at it and remember sitting on the front porch with Boyd at night talking about girls from school or about what we were going to do with our lives when we got older. Boyd knew even then that he was going to be on the radio. It's all he ever wanted to do. I wasn't that sure about what I wanted to do. I really didn't have any idea at all.

"I'll listen to you on the radio," I said to Boyd. "No matter what, I'll do that."

*

My first radio was a transistor radio that came with a leather case and an earplug. I got the radio for selling 50 boxes

147

of greeting cards door-to-door. I was eleven at the time, and the town we lived in was very flat so I could pick up radio stations from all over the country at night. During the day, I could only get a station 20 miles away, but at night, I could hear everything.

*

The radio I own now picks up very few stations. The clearest one I can get features organ music of the kind that they played at roller rinks, bouncy music. In one of the towns where we lived, a resort town on a lake with an amusement park, there was a roller rink with bouncy music. I skated there on Saturday afternoons in the summer. In the winter, the roller rink closed down. So did the rides and the caramel apple stand, the root beer place and the gift shops. In the summer, I skated every week because I had a crush on a girl who also skated every Saturday. I wanted to be such a good skater that she would stop to watch me. Then she would fall in love with me and we would skate together to the bouncy music, which was played by a woman named Janet Baish. Janet Baish sat at the organ in an elevated alcove at one end of the rink and swayed back and forth while she played. She wore glasses and always a dress with sleeves. Her hair was pulled into a tight bun but, by the end of the day, especially on hot days, it would start to unspool and slip to one side of her head. At the other end of the rink was a counter where you got your skates and could buy bottles of pop and candy bars. One of the long walls between Janet Baish and the counter was covered in mirrors and the other had wide-screened windows where people walking past could look in. The girl I had a crush on never stopped to watch me skate or join me. The only time she looked my way was when I lost my balance and clattered futilely before falling to the floor, smacking the back of my head.

I'm not sure I'll keep this radio. I have the one in car and it works, and, when I get to Tucumcari, I'm betting Audrey has something better, maybe hooked up to stereo speakers and a tall tower on the roof of her house. I'll probably be able to hear stations from one coast to the other, Canada to Mexico.

*

Even if it wasn't time for Boyd's program to be on, whenever I was traveling, driving for work or to a new place for a new job, I listened to the radio in the car. I liked to listen to the little stations in the towns I drove through or past. I liked listening to the announcers talk about a sale at the men's clothing store and read the school hot lunch menu. The announcers weren't as good as Boyd but their hearts were in it, you could tell. They loved their towns. They loved to talk to people in their towns. I'd guess they were pretty famous in their communities. I'd guess everybody knew them by name. Most of what they talked about was happy. Not much bad happens in those places. Somebody's house might catch fire, of course, or there might be a car accident involving teenagers drinking after a school dance or a football game, but those were rare, and when they did happen, there was genuine sadness in the voices of the announcers because they knew the people whose tragedies they were reporting. Once, just after I heard about an accident where a popular high school girl—a senior and a cheerleader—was killed when her car rolled over, I met the funeral procession. The cars following the hearse stretched for miles. I stopped to let them pass and watched until the last one had turned into the cemetery.

*

I pull up next to the curb in front of Boyd's house and park. Before I get out, I look up and down the street for a car that might belong to Osseo Fairchild, but all of the cars here look like they belong. They are washed and waxed, so shiny the world is reflected along their doors and in their hubcaps. In this part of the city, upwind from the factories and their smokestacks, the ash is not as thick or constant, so it's possible to keep a car clean. Mine is the only one that looks out of place, the only one streaked and caked with gray and sitting next to the curb in its own cloud.

*

When I get out of my car, a man across the street waves at me. He is kneeling on his lawn digging out dandelions then tossing them into a black plastic bucket. He looks up and waves at me with his digging tool. He waggles it at me and smiles. I smile and wave back. I think about saying something to him about the nice weather or how pesky dandelions can be, but I don't want to get caught in a conversation right now, so I turn back to my car and lock the door. By the time it dawns on me to ask the man if he'd seen anybody else stop by here this morning, he's already up and walking around the corner of his house. His bucket looks full.

There is no one else out. In either direction, the yards are empty.

*

I wonder if I should be here. I wonder if I'm doing the right thing. I wonder if there's any way to know.

*

All I can hear is my heart. Then all I can hear is the scrape of my shoes on the sidewalk, on the concrete steps up to Boyd's front door. Then, after I stop, my heart again.

I ring the bell and can hear someone moving inside.

*

Boyd comes to the door dragging an oxygen bottle on wheels.

He thinks I am a fan. In the hand not pulling the little oxygen tank, he is holding a picture of himself, the same one he sent to me. He pushes the screen door open a crack and slides it through to me.

"Thanks for stopping by," he says in a ragged whisper. "I appreciate it."

"I have one of these," I say.

"That's okay," he says. "Thanks again for stopping by." He starts to push the door closed, but I put my hand on it and hold it open. "What are you doing?"

"You're coming with me," I tell him.

"Why would I go with you?"

"Because I'm Osseo Fairchild."

*

Boyd comes to the door dragging an oxygen bottle on wheels. He is hunched over, caved in around his chest, and he moves slowly.

I tell Boyd who I am. I tell him I used to live here.

"I'm sorry," he says in his raspy voice, "I don't remember you."

I point up the street to where the porch of my old house

can be seen beneath the leaves of a eucalyptus tree.

"That's Mickey Peck's house," he says.

"Hey," I say, grinning, "remember the time I got stuck in the mud in your grandmother's garden?"

"That's wasn't you. That was Mickey Peck. I used to tell that story all the time on the radio, that's where you got it."

"It wasn't Mickey Peck. It was me. I don't even know Mickey Peck."

He says something I can't hear and waves a hand at me, shooing me away.

"The socks," I remind him. "The socks I was wearing were gray and they had a brown design on the ankles."

"They had chess pieces. They were knights. I mentioned them on the radio, too."

"I know. I heard you tell about the garden and the socks, but you never ever got it right. You always said it was Mickey Peck, but it was me."

"I'm really sorry, but I've got to go now. Thanks for stopping by. It was nice seeing you again."

When Boyd starts to push the inside door closed, I open the screen door and stop him. He pushes harder and tries to force me back, but he is not very strong anymore.

"What are you doing?" he asks. His face is starting to turn blue from pushing and I am afraid he is going to die right now.

"I'm here to take you away," I tell him. "I'm going to take you with me."

"You're going to—why would I go with you?"

"Because," I say to him, "I'm going to save your life."

*

A woman in a white dress comes to the door. When she opens the door, I see that her dress is a uniform. She is a nurse.

I tell her who I am. I point out my house. I ask to see Boyd.

"I'm sorry," she says, sounding sorry. "But Mr. Delmarco can't see anyone right now. Can I give him your phone number so he can call you when he's feeling up to it?"

*

A woman in a white dress comes to the door. She listens to me with her arms wrapped around herself. I can tell that she can't understand me. I can tell because the look on her face is the same look my students used to have when I gave them a new word to learn, a new phrase. I ask her if I can see Boyd. I speak slowly and clearly. I know she understands me this time, but she shakes her head and starts to close the door.

"Please," I say to her. "I just want to talk to him for a minute."

She shakes her head again.

"No, no," she says. "Mr. Boyd, he dead."

154

The man who reads the Bible on the radio disappears suddenly, without warning. Everything in the tin building is just as he left it: his chair, the microphone, headphones. Once the round-faced boy discovers that all he can pick up on the radio is static, he is heart-broken. He has trouble sleeping, and when he wakes up from terrifying dreams, he opens his mouth to scream but no sound comes out. Plagued by insomnia and lack of appetite, the round-faced boy becomes wispy and fragile. His clothes become the clothes of a much larger boy. His skin turns waxy, yellow. His eyes hurt in the sunlight and pour out tears at night. Finally, after a long time has passed but having never given up, the boy hears a sound behind the static, a voice faint but familiar. "I'm still here," the voice says. "I'm still here."

Saving Boyd

The woman who comes to the door, it turns out, is not a nurse at all. She is a cleaning woman, and she used to be one of my students. She recognizes me and says, "Mister Teacher," which is what I taught them to call me. "How have you been?" Which is something else I taught them.

In her imperfect English, she reminds me that her name is Da-Fonte. She tells me she works for a company that hires immigrants and gives them jobs as maids or gardeners. Some of my other former students work for this same company or a company just like it. They used to tell me that their employer paid them poorly, made them buy their own uniforms, and kept them from complaining by saying government people would come and get them and send them back to the country they came from if they caused any trouble. A lot of them told me they would steal from the homes where they cleaned or cut the grass, just to survive. They knew they would get sent back if they ever got caught, but what choice did they have?

Da-Fonte takes my arm and smiles. Her teeth are broad and flat and very white, whiter even than her cleaning woman uniform. She takes my arm and brings me inside. She brings me inside and she makes me stand next to the door. This is the living room of Boyd's house. The living room is carpeted but I am standing on a little piece of tiled floor between the door and the stairway that leads to the second floor of Boyd's house. This is where Da-Fonte wants me to stand. She holds up her hand to keep me there and then she goes into another room. I want to follow her and look the place over to see if I think I remember anything, but I don't. I stay put between the door and the stairway. Boyd's living room is filled with furniture and boxes. All of the pictures have been taken off the wall. Mirrors, too. The rugs are rolled up and tied. Lampshades are stacked one on top of another on the couch. Glass doors on a china cabinet are taped shut. The name of a moving company is printed on the boxes and each one is labeled in large black letters: *Dishes, Canned Goods, Books, Books, Glass—Be Careful!, Towels, Basement.* There is a smell of dust and pine-scented cleaner in the air, and there is a stillness, too. It is the stillness that comes with death.

*

When my father died, when we were living in the little house that overlooked the ocean and he died in his bed there, the air

157

was so still that I could hear my mother's tears hit the floor. When she let go of his hand and stood up to go call the funeral home, all of the sounds of the world came back: the waves on the rocks, the sea gulls, traffic on the highway, a barking dog, the dialing of the phone.

I stood in the doorway and looked at my father in his bed with his arms folded across his stomach and his face turned away from me, and I remember thinking how thin he had gotten, how thin and brittle. I remember thinking how radiation had burned up most of him and left only this remnant, this skeleton with gray paper skin. He was so light then, so free of gravity, it was no wonder his soul left him. There was hardly anything left to keep it caged in, so it took off and rode his last breath out over the ocean and up into the sky and up even higher.

Maybe that's not exactly what I was thinking when I looked at my father in that bed.

I was only eleven at the time.

Eleven, going on twelve.

*

Da-Fonte comes back with a newspaper and hands it to me. It is opened and folded back so that the story about Boyd is all I see. There is a photograph with the story. It is the photograph he sent out to all of his fans and to me.

Da-Fonte motions for me to sit, flapping one arm up and down. A man's gold watch slides out from under the short sleeve of her uniform and stops at her elbow. She pushes it back up again out of sight and pushes me toward the stairway until I sit down on one of the lower steps.

"Read," she says, "read here. This," and then she leaves me again, disappearing into another room. A vacuum cleaner starts up.

Here's what I learn from the newspaper:

Boyd died two days ago in the hospital. He had been there for almost a month in a coma. He had no living relatives. When he died, there was no one there at his bedside.

*

Once, Boyd had four guests on his program to talk about what happens to us after we die. One of the guests was a minister who said people go to heaven, which he said has gold streets and is very sunny all the time with a light breeze. In the middle of heaven is the tree that got Adam and Eve in trouble. After you die, you can pick all the apples you want.

Another guest said she could communicate with people who had already died, and they filled her in on what it was like. These dead people described the afterlife as a place made up of spheres, and you went to whichever sphere your life on earth earned for

159

you. You didn't have to stay there, though, because the Universal Law of Progress lets you move to better spheres by owning up to the bad things you did while you were alive. Decent folk, she said, start out in the third sphere, which is called Summerland, and they all turn into themselves at age 21 or 22.

The third guest said when you die, that's it. You are, and then you aren't anymore. This guest was a philosophy professor from a famous university.

The fourth guest was a scientist who had written a book that used physics to prove there was immortality. He used formulas and models to show that, because all of us came from the same proton that started the universe, we are, always have been, and always will be, alive. The proton, he said, is God, meaning that the whole universe and everything in it, including us, is God, too, in a way.

The scientist didn't really get to talk too much about what it was like to be immortal because the woman who communicated with the dead kept interrupting him. She interrupted all of the other guests, and Boyd, too.

When the program ended, Boyd thanked everyone and said he didn't know which one of their stories was true, but, like everybody else, he'd know someday.

*

I unfold and then re-fold the newspaper so that the front page is showing and lay it on the step next to me.

This kind of thing has happened to me before, some surprise or a disappointment I didn't count on. I don't ever seem to be able to see it coming, but I try not to let it bother me too much. I have other plans, other ways to go. It'll work out. In the end, it always seems to work out.

In the other room, Da-Fonte vacuums wildly, banging the machine into chairs and walls. I can hear from the sound of the wheels when she runs the machine off the edge of the rug and onto the wood floor. I can hear her voice very softly through the motor's whine. I think she might be singing. Maybe she's praying.

*

Da-Fonte is always sent to houses where someone has died. Before she came to this city, when she was still living in a tiny village in the mountains of her own country, she learned from her mother and her aunts how to tend to the dead. They taught her what oils keep the skin moist and what spices work best to keep away the odor of decay. They taught her how to bind a jaw closed and how to puncture a tiny hole in an eardrum to let the person's soul escape. She learned the special prayers that would help the soul find its way to heaven and the special prayers that would keep her from being haunted by souls reluctant to leave this world.

Da-Fonte's older sister, Tempra, was also taught the secrets of preparing the dead, but she refused to believe the stories about reluctant souls. Her mother and her aunts and even Da-Fonte warned her not to be foolish, but she would not listen to them. When a man in their village who kept canaries died, Tempra was sent to his house. She did everything she had been taught to do except recite the prayers that would protect her. Because the man had died suddenly, he had made no plans for the care of his canaries, so when Tempra pushed the awl through his eardrum, the man's soul, instead of floating up through the roof, clung to her like a shadow and began whispering to her, telling her what she needed to do for the birds. Realizing what she had—or, rather, what she had not—done, Tempra clapped her hands over her ears and shouted out the prayer that would send the reluctant soul on its way to heaven. But it was too late. The canary man could not be dismissed. Day and night, he spoke to her, imploring her to feed his birds, to see that they had water, to look after the tiny eggs, to encourage them to sing, to keep cats away from the cages. After less than a week of torment, Tempra returned to the man's house and opened all the cages and shook them until the canaries flew away. Then, with the ghost's voice cursing her for what she had done, she ran from the village and threw herself off a cliff. She might never have been found were it not for the song of the canaries that guided the search party to the place where the poor girl had landed. They followed the sound and found hundreds of the trilling, yellow birds perched on the rocks all around Tempra's broken body. As soon as the men arrived, the birds flew off as one, a sallow cloud.

*

Here, now, in this city, Da-Fonte can do none of the things she learned, so, instead, she cleans the houses of the deceased, putting their worldly things in order and doing what she can for any lingering spirits unable to accept their fate.

*

The second floor of Boyd's house reminds me of a house we lived in during the time my father was writing letters to the government and we were moving around a lot. That house had a long, narrow hallway with two doors on each side and a window at the end, too, but the window of that other place looked out onto bare fields—it must have been late fall; it must have been Nebraska—not the branches of a maple tree.

*

Through one of the open doors, the second one down on my left, light falls in a dusty shaft. It falls in a dusty shaft and lands on the carpet runner I am standing on.

I take it as a sign and follow the runner to the light and to the door the light falls through.

I look into the light, trying to see what's in the room. When my eyes have adjusted, what I see is Boyd.

*

Da-Fonte turns off the vacuum cleaner and I can hear her walk to the foot of the stairway. She calls up the stairs, "Mister Teacher," but I don't answer. I stand motionless and hold my breath.

A car horn sounds outside. Da-Fonte opens the front door and shouts something in her own language. Someone—a woman—shouts back and then a car door opens and closes. I hear Da-Fonte wheel the vacuum cleaner to the door. I hear the two women talking.

I hear the door close. The women's voices come now from the front of the house.

I tiptoe to the window. I stay back far enough so I can't be seen.

Da-Fonte and the other woman are lifting the vacuum cleaner into the back of a white van parked behind my car. At the passenger side door, Da-Fonte looks back at the house and touches the fingers of one hand to her forehead before getting in.

*

The man who lives across the street from Boyd's house, the man digging out dandelions, offers to help. I am making my fourth trip from the house to my car when he walks up and asks if I need a hand. I tell him that would be great.

"What's in the boxes?" he asks as we walk back to the house.

"Tapes," I tell him. "Tapes of Boyd's radio programs."

"I used to listen to him some when he was on the radio," the man says. "Not a lot, though. Mostly I listen to music."

He brushes his hand off on his pants and holds it out for me to shake.

"My name's Bob."

"Mickey," I say. "I used to live down the street when I was a kid. That house down there with the big porch. Boyd was my best friend."

Bob helps me carry the boxes from Boyd's house to my car. To get all of the boxes in my car, I have to fold down the back seat. I move my own boxes and my suitcase against the back of the front seat. When I close the back end of the station wagon, I have to push hard and carefully to get the latch to catch without crushing anything.

While we walk back and forth from the car to the house to the car, Bob tells me about the old neighborhood. He tells me about the people who have moved into the different houses and I tell him about the people who used to lived there. Bob is a very agreeable person. I like talking with him. He says a couple of things that make me laugh and I do the same. I try to imagine what it would be like to live on this street again. I think about staying in Boyd's house for a few days. Bob and I could meet out in front and talk some more. We could talk about lawns and about the teenagers who drive by with their music turned up too loud. We could watch the pretty young woman who says hello to us when she jogs past in shorts and a tank top. Bob could introduce me to his family and invite me over for dinner. He holds out his hand again for me to shake.

"Well, Mickey, it was nice meeting you. I'm just sorry it wasn't a happier time for you."

"Me, too, Bob."

Bob goes back across the street, and I get into my car.

It is evening. The sky is turning deep blue in the east and pink in the west. The shadows of trees are lengthening on the yards. I smell charcoal smoke and think about families sitting down to a supper of grilled hamburgers, sweet corn, and potato salad.

When I pull away from the curb and look in my rearview mirror, I see a swirl of ash lift off my car and then settle behind me on the street.

The atomic soldier is burning up from the inside. His body is a furnace but he is cold all of the time. He wears layers of clothing, coats over sweaters over shirts. A knit cap is pulled down low above his eyes. Even on days when the sun blazes, he shakes and his teeth chatter. At night, he wraps himself in blankets. He keeps a fire going.

The atomic soldier finds it hard to sleep. When he finally does, it is not a restful sleep. He has dreams and wakes up in a sweat that makes him even colder. He wakes up but cannot remember anything about the dreams except that they are frightening. He becomes afraid to go to sleep and stays awake, instead, next to the fire.

Finally, the lack of sleep makes him delirious, and he wanders out into the desert dragging his rusty wagon.

The young woman is looking out her kitchen window and sees a glow in the desert, a faint glow but not far away. She puts on a sweater and goes to see what it is. She comes upon the atomic soldier who is lying on his back next to his wagon. His coat has fallen open and the young woman can see, even through the sweaters and shirts, that the light is coming from inside the man, from inside his chest.

The young woman kneels next to him and then picks him up. He weighs no more than the clothes he wears. He weighs nothing at all.

My Mother's Suicide

Six months after my father died, my mother killed herself. She drove her car over a cliff. One morning, after telling me to eat my breakfast and to tidy up the kitchen, she said he had to go out. She said she would be right back. She said she would see me soon. I watched her drive away through the window over the sink. Then I finished the dishes.

I think it was a cliff. It might have been a river. It all depends where we were living at the time. I don't recall. It doesn't matter, though, because my mother came back before lunch that morning. I waved to her through the window over the sink when she pulled in.

It turns out she hadn't killed herself at all.

I was mistaken.

*

When she got older, my mother lost her memory. She was in a nursing home then, a home for the aged and the infirm. A lot of other people there had lost their memories too. I would meet them in the hallway on my way to my mother's room and they always looked puzzled, stopping me to see if I knew where they were headed, what they had to do. Most were old like my mother, but some were younger, my age, even younger. They were missing something more than just being able to remember.

My mother's room had a nice view. Just outside the window was a tree with a bird feeder. Past that, she could see a pond. When I visited, she would be sitting in a chair looking out the window. I would put my hand on her shoulder and tell her I was happy to see her. She would look up at me and frown.

"I don't know who you are," she would say, which I expected, which didn't bother me.

"I know," I would say, and she would go back to looking outside, rubbing the knuckles of one hand with the other. If there were people near the pond or beyond that on a sloping lawn, she would say, "They look like trees, walking," which was a verse from the Bible that she had always liked. She found it odd and funny. I don't think they really looked like trees to her at all. It was just something that popped into her mind at that moment.

The day my mother died, I was sitting in her chair, looking out the window, and she was in her bed right next to me. I had my hand on her hand, rubbing her knuckles with my thumb.

"Cover my feet," she said. "I don't want people looking at

my feet."

It was dark when she finally stopped breathing, and I was weightless, hovering over her, hanging on to her, not wanting to let go.

Traveling Light

Twilight lasts a long time in the summer. It lasts long enough today for me to drive out of the city and into the hills the people around here call the mountains. In this twilight, this pale pause between day and night, I climb up and away from the city, up and away from the smokestacks and the ash, up and away.

*

My father prepared me for this, the fugitive life. It's what he said we were: fugitives.

"No we're not," my mother said from her side of the front seat. "We're just rootless."

My father didn't agree with her or disagree. He flexed his fingers on the steering wheel and looked at me in the rearview mirror.

"Fugitives," he said again.

And there were times when it felt like we were fugitives, even if we weren't.

*

Once I remember two men in suits and hats coming to the house we were living in. I was sitting on the front steps with my transistor radio when they got out of their car. One of them walked past me and knocked on the door, but the other one put his hand on my head and smiled at me.

"Hey, cowboy," he said, "whatcha listening to?"

I didn't tell him, of course, because I never spoke to strangers, but I was listening to this call-in program that came on every Saturday morning right after the announcer finished reading the news. People would phone the radio station with things they wanted to sell or trade or get rid of, and then other people would call in and they'd make deals. I figured I could learn a lot about people's lives just by listening and then filling in the rest. The man who called in to sell a dollhouse he'd made himself had a daughter who wouldn't have anything to do with him, either because he drank too much or because she had run off and gotten married to an ex-convict with the tattoo of a tiger on his back. The woman with eight tabby kittens she was willing to give away to good homes because she already had more than forty cats living with her in an old house set back from the street and hidden behind overgrown lilac bushes. There were other people I listened to, too, whose stories were even more interesting, more exciting. They were stories that involved guns or jewelry or mysterious objects like honey extractors or oscilloscopes, which I'd never heard of.

That's what I was listening to through my earplug when the two men got out of their car. When my mother opened the door, I turned my radio off and followed them inside. They took their hats off and they both had blonde hair, almost white hair. They were twins. The one who had knocked on the door asked where my father was, and my mother said he was out of town on a business trip. She said he'd given her an itinerary of his trip, but lots of times he wasn't exactly where he said he'd be. It all depended on how well he was doing selling whatever it was he was selling. Cleaning products then, I think, or socket sets. My mother told them the different towns he was supposed to visit before coming home next week sometime. I knew he would be home later this very day but I didn't say anything. The one who'd called me cowboy thanked my mother and gave her a piece of paper with a phone number written on it. He asked her to have my father call that number at his earliest convenience, and then they left. When my father got home that evening and heard about the two men, he sat down and rubbed his forehead for a minute, thinking. Finally, he looked up, and I could see his eyes were red and tired.

"That's it, then," he said. "I guess we'd better get packed."

We were living somewhere very flat then, someplace where there were great stretches of prairie and a small, fenced-in herd of buffalo just outside of town. The night we left, the moon was full and the buffalo looked silver.

*

When the movers come to Boyd's house and check the list of things to load into their truck, they'll discover the boxes they expected to find in an upstairs room are gone. The police will be called in to investigate and they'll talk to Bob, who will tell them the whole story. He'll remember my car and maybe even the license plate. Another detective will call the cleaning service and talk to Da-Fonte. Then they'll start looking for me.

There will be a story in the newspaper about Boyd's tapes being stolen.

Osseo Fairchild will read the story while he's eating breakfast at a cafe not too far from Boyd's house.

He'll fold his newspaper, finish his coffee, leave a tip for the waitress on the counter, and then he'll start looking for me, too. Osseo Fairchild will come looking for me because he wants the tapes. He wants them because he feels cheated that Boyd died without his help and now he wants to destroy all that's left of the man he spent so much time hating.

Osseo Fairchild doesn't know the tapes are gone yet or who I am, so it's not him in the car behind me, the one following too closely.

But it will be him someday. Someday, I'll see a face I've never seen before behind the wheel of a car I can't remember, and I'll know he finally caught up with me.

175

*

The sun is going down, its final drop, and the highway ahead of me is wide-open, empty.

I push on the gas pedal and I am going faster than I thought I could.

I cannot feel the road, I am going so fast.

The world becomes smudges of color, then I outrun color and the world is gray, then black, and I am in space, pure light in the void, brighter than a star.

ACKNOWLEDGEMENTS

I am grateful to a number of people who have, over the years and in its various permutations, read and advised me on the manuscript that is now this novel: Rachael Stewart, Eugene Baldwin, Richard Gage, Deb Brod, Joanie O'Leary, Marta Walz, Angela Ogburn Landers, Carole Maso, Philip Dacey, Joe Hurka, Maureen McCoy, Marc Petersen, Amy Lerman, Richard Hollinger and Scott Elledge. My appreciation for and gratitude to three writers—Richard Jones, David Jauss and Michael Martone—whose work I greatly admire and who were kind enough to read my book and say nice things about it. To Jesi Buell and the staff at KERNPUNKT: thank you for liking Tucumcari enough to publish it and for being so good at your jobs. Teagan Studebaker, *go raibh maith agat*, for the website home page photo. To offspring Andrew and Elise, much obliged for your putting up with me, and, lastly, an unending "thanks a million" to my wife, Beth, who is and always will be my best reader, my best friend, my best everything.

Patrick Parks has had fiction published in a variety of journals, including *The Chattahoochee Review*, *The Beloit Fiction Journal*, *Clockwatch Review*, *Farmer's Market*, and *B City*, and had a story in the anthology, The Breast. In addition, he was editor of *Black Dirt*, *a literary journal*, edited *Sarajevo: An Anthology for Bosnian Relief*, and wrote reviews for *Literary Magazine Review*. Recipient of two Illinois Arts Council awards, he is a graduate of the University of Iowa's Writers' Workshop. He lives with his wife on the train line near Chicago.

Photo by Elizabeth Parks